Cage of Invisible Bars

Dawn Merriman

Dedication

I can't write any of these books without the support of my wonderful husband, Kevin and my children. A special thank you to Belinda Martin for all her help, brainstorming sessions and overall support.

-Dawn Merriman

Chapter 1

SHERIFF KINGSLEY

With the blood stains on her face and the mud caked in her yellow curls, the young woman on the other side of the interrogation table looks older than I know she is. Her eyes seem ancient. The dark blue is striking, but the sadness behind them, tears at my heart.

"Where's Aster?" the young woman asks, the startling blue eyes darting around the tiny interrogation room. "You won't hurt her, will you? She doesn't understand any of this."

I assure her Aster is fine and being looked after in a different part of the sheriff's office.

"Are you thirsty?" I take one of the water

bottles sitting between us and twist off the top. Her fingers shake as she reaches for the bottle. One of the nails has been torn off to the quick, the pink rawness bright against the grime wedged under the other nails.

She accepts the bottle, but runs a dirty fingernail along the label, pushes the side as if to test the plastic. The bottle seems to scare her and she eyes it mistrustfully. The tip of her tongue runs along her cracked lips in anticipation.

"It's water, Nellie," I say gently. "It's only water. It won't hurt you."

She tips the bottle to her lips and sips cautiously. Her eyes lock on mine as if challenging my assertion the water is safe.

I nod slightly and she closes her eyes and gulps the water until the bottle is empty. It crackles under her grip.

"So sweet," she says, wiping a drop off her chin and setting the empty bottle on the table between us. She looks at me quickly, ashamed. "I'm sorry I didn't share it with you." She bows her head, suddenly miserable. "That was selfish of me."

I watch the quick change come over her, baffled. "That's completely okay. We have lots more water bottles." I choose one of the remaining bottles for myself and take a drink.

She raises her head, eyeing me skeptically. "How? He said there was nothing like that left. We only had water out of the creek. I'd have to boil it before we drank it and even then it always tasted like mud."

I nearly choke on the water in my mouth. "Jack told you a lot of things that weren't true. You'll learn as we go."

"Where's Aster? She'll want some water."

"Aster has had water already. I'm sure she loved it."

This brings a smile to her cracked lips. "That girl loves anything sweet. You should see her eat berries. She shoves them in so fast her lips end up all stained with red. I have to scrub her hard to get her clean before Jack comes home."

"Did Jack leave often?"

"Nearly every day. Sometimes at night."

"You never thought to leave?"

Her head whips in my direction so fast tiny pieces of caked on mud fly from her curls and skitter across the table.

"Why would I leave? That was my home. He warned me that the world was different, dangerous. If I left the woods, Aster and I would get hurt."

"He threatened to hurt you?"

She shakes her head and more mud sprinkles on the table. "Staying at the cabin kept us safe. He said people out here would hurt us. Especially people like you." She motions to my badge.

"The police? We would hurt you?"

"The world was chaos, he said. Many people had died, and those that were left scrambled to survive."

I rub my hand across my mustache in disgust. She believes every word she's saying, every lie Jack fed her.

"So you stayed to keep safe?"

She nods earnestly.

"But here we are now. What changed?"

She thinks about the question for a long time before she answers. "It all started when I found the doll. It was floating in the creek. It had been burned and was missing half its hair, but I thought Aster would like it. Her third birthday was coming up and I wanted to give her something special."

Her voice trails off and I give her a moment to collect her thoughts.

"How did the doll change things?"

She shrugs and says, "It just did." There's a lot more to the doll than she's ready to tell me.

"Take your time."

She looks around the room again as if Aster will suddenly appear. "Bring Aster to me and I'll tell you everything you want to know."

Nellie's blue eyes bore into mine, daring me to refuse her. I've stared down hardened criminals and the dregs of society with more ease than I can stare down this teenage mother. The decision is easy, I don't want to tell her no.

Opening the interrogation room door a crack, I ask for Aster to be brought in. "And bring me some bottles of Pepsi. Oh, and some chocolate."

Nellie's smile of anticipation brings a matching smile to my lips. "If you like water, wait to you try Pepsi and chocolate," I tell her.

"We had chocolate once. Last Christmas."

My smile fades at the words.

We had chocolate once. No one in Maddison, Indiana, or anywhere, for that matter, should be forced to live a life where those words cross your lips.

"While we wait for Aster, why don't you start at the beginning.

"I don't remember the beginning."

"Then start where you need to start. Where did you get the chocolate at Christmas?"

"Jack brought it. He brought us everything we have."

"Where did he get things? Did he have a job, did he make money somehow?"

The question confuses her. "Jack says there is no money anymore."

Another sentence I didn't expect to hear.

"Then tell me about the doll."

Chapter 2

NELLIE

Thankfully, there is some of yesterday's oatmeal left so I don't have to start a fire in the wood burning stove to make breakfast for Jack and Aster. The sun is barely up, but the heat in the cabin is already pressing on my skin. I've opened all the windows as well as the front and back doors, but there's no breeze to offer relief.

A cold breakfast will have to suffice today.

I know Aster won't complain. My precious girl rarely complains or whines about anything. I look across the cramped cabin to where she sleeps on her cot in the corner. She's thrown her cover off in the heat and her face is flushed. One pudgy toddler arm hangs off the

13

cot wearing a fresh pattern of pink mosquito bites. Late August in the cabin is brutal with both heat and bugs. It almost makes me yearn for winter.

Almost.

As I watch my daughter sleep, I absently scratch at my shoulder, a fresh bite of my own itching.

The precious moment is shattered when the door to the only bedroom opens, and Jack strides out. "You got coffee made yet?" he grumbles.

Coffee in this heat?

"I wasn't going to start a fire this morning because it's so hot." Jack looks at me like I've said something incredibly stupid. "But I can make some if you like," I hurriedly add.

He towers over me and stares, blinking slowly, not needing to say a word.

"I'll go get some water."

I grab the water pail and head for the creek, happy to escape to the outdoors. I don't let Jack's grumbling mood bother me. He's always testy in the mornings. He'd said last night that he was going out scavenging today. I should have remembered. I should have planned a better morning than cold oatmeal and plain water.

I hurry down the path to the creek, the dried grass cracking under my bare feet, the morning sun baking into my shoulders.

The sooner I get Jack fed, the sooner he can leave.

I instantly feel guilty for the thought. Jack provides for Aster and I and keeps us safe. He is our entire world, the only other person we ever see. I should be grateful for all he does for us. I should take better care of him.

No coffee? What were you thinking?

I kneel on the bank of the creek, the small stones digging into my knees. Reaching into the water, I dip my pail into the clearest part of the creek. I'm careful to only touch water, not the bottom, or floating leaves. If I stir the creek up, I have to move upstream a bit and try again. As I dip the pail, a mosquito lands on my face and I instinctively swat at it. The pail touches the bottom and kicks up muddy sediment.

"Flip it," I exclaim, angry that I let myself be distracted from a chore I've done a thousand times. The water swirls with brown from the bottom.

It's too dirty to drink now.

Frustrated with myself and the incessant bugs, I climb to my feet and walk a few steps upstream. At this time of year, the creek is low, only a few inches deep in some places. It's difficult to find a good dipping place. My favorite spot won't be clear again for a few minutes, and I don't want to make Jack wait.

Something blue in the branches along the creek bed catches my eye. At first, I think its simple trash, a plastic bag or an empty bottle. The creek often brings treasures from upstream. When you have as little as we do, anything new is a blessing. A ripple of excitement pulses through me as I push through the bushes to reach the blue thing. Once I grow closer, I see it's not blue trash at all, it's a doll wearing a torn blue dress.

"What a darling doll," I exclaim, untangling

the doll's lace hem from the branch that has it pinned to the edge of the creek. The doll is half-burned and some of its hair has been singed off, but I know I can make something lovely out of it. I rub at the burn marks and mud on the doll's plastic skin, some of it wipes away.

Excited now, I dip my pail quickly, yet carefully, then hurry back to show Jack my find.

I burst into the cabin, full of excitement. I find him where I often find him. Looking into the wooden box on a shelf in the kitchen. He's obsessed with the box and looks in it often. Sometimes he reaches in and rifles through the contents. I once looked inside and found only some small animal bones. The thing disgusted me. Why keep animal bones in a box on a shelf? I never asked, and I never cared. If the box made Jack happy, then that was in my best interest.

Jack notices my presence and drops the lid. It slams shut with a clunk.

"What you got there, Nellie?" He has the

look of being caught doing something wrong. I don't understand. He can fondle his stupid animal bones if he wants. I don't care. I'm more interested in the doll.

"I found this doll in the creek," I whisper, darting a look towards Aster to make sure she's still sleeping.

"It's an ugly thing," Jack says. "You should throw it back."

I hold the doll to my chest. "I'm not throwing it back. I thought I'd clean it up and give it to Aster for her birthday next week."

Jack's brief interest has waned already. "Do what you like," he says and goes outside. "Let me know when the coffee is ready."

I'm so fascinated by the doll, I forgot about the coffee. "A new dress, fix your hair, clean your face. You'll be the nicest toy Aster ever had."

Hearing her name, Aster shifts in her cot. I don't want her to see the doll, not yet. I run into the bedroom I share with Jack and place the doll carefully under the bed.

"Mama?" Aster calls sleepily.

I hate to leave the doll behind, want to start fixing her up, but my daughter needs me.

"Right here, baby." I go to the counter where I left the water pail. "You hungry?"

Aster toddles from her cot to me, scratching at the bites on her arm. "Uh, huh." She leans into my leg, wanting a snuggle. Her dark curls tickle my bare skin.

"I'll hold you in a minute. Jack needs his coffee."

I put small sticks of wood and some dry tinder in the stove and light it with the long stick lighter that Jack brought home years ago. I pull on the trigger a few times, but it refuses to light. Jack walks in while I'm trying to get the fire started and sees me struggling.

"That lighter's about dead. I'll have to find you a new one soon."

"Da-Da," Aster exclaims.

My back goes stiff. Aster is always excited to see Jack, too young to understand that he barely tolerates her. She gobbles any scrap of attention she gets from him. "Is your bed dry?" he asks stiffly.

I started potty training Aster as soon as she was old enough. She spent most of the summer outside anyway and it wasn't that hard to train her to drop her pants and go. The outhouse is a horrid place in the summer, so I didn't force her to use it except for when necessary. As with anything I teach Aster, she learned quickly. Now she only occasionally has accidents, and only at night. The occasional wet bed annoys Jack to no end.

"All dry," Aster answers brightly.

I pull the trigger on the stick lighter a few more times, hoping Jack will say something encouraging, something positive.

"Good girl," he says.

The lighter lights and the tinder jumps to life. With the small fire going and Jack in a good mood, I set to heating the water and making the coffee. Aster runs outside to do her business.

Jack sits heavily in a chair at the wooden table. The old chair creaks under his considerable weight. "I might not make it home tonight," he says. "Getting harder to find things around here. Most places have been picked over pretty well already."

Jack says this nearly every day, but I smile and act interested.

Jack continues, "You are so lucky you get to stay here and be safe. It's a dangerous place out there, even for a man like me who can handle himself."

The coffee is finally done and I hand Jack his cup. His large hand dwarfs the blue ceramic mug. Bowing my head slightly, I say by rote, "We appreciate all you do for us." I learned the hard way that Jack is fairly easy to please. He likes me to always say thank you, and he likes things to be clean and tidy. He likes me to remember at all times that I owe him my life.

He never lets me forget that one.

"Might be gone until tomorrow night if I need to find you a new lighter, too," he adds.

"We will miss you while you are gone," I say, my eyes cast down, focusing on his boots that I wiped down for him last night. Clean and neat, I know my job.

"Da-Da, don't go," Aster says, bouncing in

the back door suddenly.

Jack swivels in the chair, and the chair groans in protest. "Do you like to eat?" he snaps.

Aster nods, fear growing in her eyes, knowing she crossed a line.

"Then I need to go find you food." He darts his eyes to me then fixes them on Aster again. I move towards her protectively, my feet crossing the wood plank floor of their own accord. I take her slight shoulders in my hands. "We appreciate how hard you work," I say in my most submissive voice, giving Aster's shoulders a prompting squeeze.

"Thank you for all our food, Da-Da."

"Don't you forget that everything you have comes from me."

Aster nods again, her fingers slipping into her mouth, a self-soothing act she rarely does now.

Everything comes from Jack.

Everything except the doll hiding under the bed.

Chapter 3

NELLIE

It's cooler under the trees than in the cabin, so Aster and I spend as much time as possible outside. I have covered her tender skin in mud to protect it from the bug bites. She looks adorable running around in shorts and a tank top, with feet bare and covered in a layer of mud. Even her face has mud on it. Her hair is curly like mine, but dark brown like Jack's. She's brown from head to toe. Even her eyes are brown, but the darkness of them break the monotony of the color.

"Brown like a muskrat," Aster says looking at the mud caked on her. "Mama brown, too?"

I wasn't planning to mud myself, but Aster's suggestion seems like a good one. I pull more handfuls from the edge of the creek and rub it on my bare arms. The mud feels cool and soothing. "I'm brown like a muskrat, too." I tell her. I reach for another handful of mud, ready to cover my legs.

The animal across the creek is not a muskrat.

It's a dog.

A big black dog.

Half-crouched, heart pounding, with nothing but a handful of mud as a weapon, I tell Aster to get behind me.

"Black doggy," Aster says, peaking from behind my legs. "Come here doggy."

"Quiet," I tell her. "We don't know what it wants."

The dog doesn't know what it wants either. It doesn't growl or raise its hair at us. It just sits down on its haunches, cocks its head and looks at us quietly.

"Go away," I tell it.

"No, Mama, I want the doggy."

The dog doesn't seem to be threatening, but it has been years since I've seen a dog so I can't be sure. All I have is vague recollections of a brown, long eared thing that lived with me in my previous life. Aster has never seen a dog in real life, only in the books Jack brings home.

"Go away," I tell the dog again, mud dripping thorough my tightly clenched fingers.

It only whines and lowers her head to her paws.

"Come here, doggy," Aster says, stepping from behind my legs. "Come play."

The dog scoots on her belly towards us, a sure sign of submission. The dog's brown eyes search my face.

"You're hungry, aren't you?"

The dog makes a whining sound of anticipation.

I remember something way back in my past, "Wanna treat?"

The dog springs to her feet and dances in a circle.

Aster giggles with delight. "Do again, Mama."

"Treat, wanna treat?" I repeat. The dog dances again.

Overcome with excitement and hunger, the

dog bounds across the creek, splashing us with water, washing off some of the carefully applied mud. The black furry thing, rubs against Aster, careful not to knock her down. Aster squeals and laughs.

My heart swells with the sound. I have no idea what we'll do with a dog or how Jack will react to its presence. He said he won't be home until tomorrow, so I have time to figure it out.

"Treat?" Aster asks the dog and it spins for her.

"Let's go see if we can find some lunch for it, and for us." The three of us make our way to the cabin. Supplies are low, hence the big run Jack is on today, but I'm sure I can scrounge us up something to eat.

Aster is too busy watching the dog to eat much, but the animal scarfs down whatever I give her.

After lunch, with a stern warning to keep close to the cabin, Aster takes the dog outside to play. The dog seems friendly enough, but its back is as high as Aster's chest and I worry it might hurt her if it gets to playing too rough. I watch from the open back door and realize I didn't have to worry. Aster simply sits on the ground and the dog lies down next to her. She prattles on about little girl things while pulling clumps of grass and weeks out of the ground and sprinkling it on the dog's back.

I wonder why Jack never found us a dog. A dog is good company and it's also good protection. In the years before Aster was born, I was so lonely when Jack would leave, I'd have loved to have a dog for a friend. I did try to make friends with a mouse that lived in the cabin. The mouse "listened" as I talked, desperate for a friend. But that was the extent of that relationship. After a while the mouse disappeared. I liked to pretend he found himself a mouse wife and went off to have dozens of mouse babies. I knew he probably got eaten by a hawk or a mink, or some other animal.

I don't have the heart to think about what Jack will say when he sees the dog. He said he'll be gone until tomorrow, so I decide to enjoy her visit while it lasts.

With Aster fully entertaining herself, I finally have a chance to take a good look at the doll I found this morning. On mud covered knees, I flip back the thin cover on our bed and look for the doll. I must have put it under the bed with more force than I thought, because it is all the way in the far corner, pushed up against the wall. Our room is so small, there is only room for a bed pushed in a corner and a four drawer dresser to hold all our clothes.

I reach for the doll, but can't quite catch it. Lying on my belly, I shimmy under the bed, surprised at the dust bunnies and the spider webs. Making a mental note to clean under here before Jack sees it, I stretch out my arm and manage to snag the doll by its hair.

Sliding backwards, I bring the doll out into the light. After a quick check on Aster to make sure she and the dog are still playing nice outside, I sit on the floor and inspect the doll.

Her hair was once blond and curled like mine. Part of it is burned off and what remains is a matted mess. I pull a few twigs and leaves out of it. I might be able to tame the curls into some semblance of hair, or worst case, I can cut off what is left and Aster's doll can just have short hair.

Her melted face is another matter. The doll's eyes are painted on, but one is melted and looks like it's wearing a horrid mask. "A little paint and I can fix that," I say with good intentions. Secretly, I know it will take more than paint to cover the melted plastic, but I don't think Aster will mind too much. I'll just explain that her doll is "special" and she will love it.

The rest of the doll is in pretty good shape. It's dirty, but I'm really good at cleaning. The blue dress is torn and filthy. I'm fairly good at fixing small holes and patches in our clothes, but I'm not a whiz with the needle and thread. All of our clothes come from things Jack finds on his scavenging runs.

I get an idea and with another quick check on Aster to be sure she won't walk in on the surprise, I dig out the box of baby clothes tucked under her cot. Jack may not be the friendliest of men, but he likes his girls to look pretty. He often brought home cute dresses and outfits for Aster, not that she had anywhere to wear them. During the days I let her run around in play clothes. I'm always careful to have us both as properly bathed as possible with creek water and dressed in our finest by the time Jack returns in the evenings.

Jack would have a fit if he saw us how we are now, covered in mud.

The box of baby clothes holds a few dresses that will work. I choose a bright pink one, Aster's favorite color and one of Jack's favorite dresses.

After cleaning up the doll, cutting its hair short and even and dressing it in the pink dress, she doesn't look too bad. I still have to figure something to do about her melted eye, but compared to how she looked pulled straight from the creek, it's a huge improvement.

I hear Aster coming so I quickly hide the doll in a cabinet and shut the door just as she barrels in with the dog hot on her heels.

"Look, mama."

Apparently Aster was playing some dress up

of her own. The dog has dandelions and weeds tucked into its fur. Most of the flowers have fallen out already, but it's obvious what she was trying to do.

"Wow, she looks beautiful," I croon.

Aster beams. "I call her Grass."

"Yes, some of that is grass." As I watch, grass and weeds fall onto the cabin floor.

"No, doggy is called Grass. I named her."

I've never heard of a dog named Grass before, but then again I don't know any other dogs either.

"Grass is a nice name," I say, privately thinking, Daisy would have been a better choice, or even clover. She has all of those things on her.

"Come, Grass. Let's go run."

Aster sprints from the back door to the front door and back outside, leaving dried mud, grass and weeds on the floor. I check the sun to gauge the time. I have a few hours until dark. I've already done most of the daily chores. A quick run around with the broom and I sweep out the mess Aster drug in. I dig out the dust bunnies from under our bed, and sweep out under Aster's cot for good measure.

Aster and Grass run around outside and with nothing pressing to do, I sit on the front steps and watch them. My brown little girl and the black dog make quiet a pair. I say a quick prayer that Jack might surprise us and let us keep the dog. By the time he comes home tomorrow, Aster will be heartbroken if she has to let Grass go away.

Go away where?

Where did the dog come from? She's much too sweet and well behaved to be a mongrel stray that Jack says roam the streets now. She seems like someone's pet.

Who has pets? Everyone is barely scraping by, according to Jack. The world outside our woods is full of chaos and danger.

Grass doesn't seem to come from that world. Where did she come from?

Chapter 4

NELLIE

Scrubbed clean of the day's mud and dressed in a fresh night shirt, I let Aster sleep with Grass on her cot. They both seemed delighted at the arrangement. After Aster is fast asleep, I sneak the doll out of the cabinet where I'd hidden her earlier. The pink dress looks good, and the hair is as neatly trimmed as possible, but the melted eye still freaks me out to look at.

Jack once brought home some paints for Aster to play with. Maybe I can use them to paint on a more suitable face. The doll may not look wonderful, but it's the only doll Aster has ever seen, so I don't think she will mind too much.

The paints are stored on a shelf near Aster's cot. Leaving the doll on the table, I quietly sneak into the storage section of the cabin that is also Aster's sleeping area. Until recently, her cot was in Jack and I's room, tucked into the only open corner. It made things easier for when she woke at night as a baby.

"She's too old to sleep with us," Jack had said one morning. He'd then unceremoniously dragged the cot into the open storage area.

A thin wall was all that separated me from my daughter at night, but it might as well have been an ocean. Sometimes I can hear her sniffling in the dark on the other side of the wall. I'll put my hand on the wall and send comfort through the planks. On nights when Jack is out late, I sometimes let Aster into bed with me. I sing nonsense songs and tell her stories until she falls asleep. I'm always careful not to fall asleep myself. If Jack finds me in bed with her, he won't be happy. He wants me all to himself.

Tonight, Aster didn't want me to sing or tell her a story. Tonight she just wanted Grass with her.

I move some items around on the shelf, careful not to disturb her. The light from the candle on the table barely reaches this corner of the cabin, but it reflects off of Grass's eyes as she watches me warily.

With her tiny charge asleep, the dog is on high alert, even protecting her from me. The intense brown eyes locked on my every move make me a little uncomfortable. Thankfully, it doesn't take long to find the paints I was looking for. I hurry the few steps back to the table, feeling the dog's eyes on me the whole way.

I focus on painting a passable replacement eye on the doll, and even touch up her lips. Once finished, I sit the doll up and survey my handiwork. She doesn't look half-bad. Aster's birthday is soon. I'm not sure exactly when, I'll have to ask Jack. I have a hard time keeping track of time here in the woods. The day of the week doesn't matter a bit. Jack comes and goes on his own schedule and Aster and I's days are filled with the same chores, same meal, same scrubbing down at night in the creek.

The irony that Jack expects us both to be

clean while he is home, but I only have access to dirty creek water to clean with is not lost on me. If it rains and the creek gets a bunch of run-off, the water turns a pale brown. I have to collect it, and let the silt and mud settle to the bottom before I can use it. Sometimes I feel dirtier after scrubbing up than I did before.

I never tell Jack this. For him, it's the ritual, the obedience.

"Cleanliness is next to Godliness," he always says.

This cabin is full of clean, but I don't know how much God is here.

If it's really raining, and Jack isn't home, Aster and I strip naked and bathe in the downpour. No matter how cold it is, she loves those times. She runs around the small clearing round the cabin, splashing in the puddles in the grass. If the puddles are extra deep, she lies down and pretends to swim across the yard. She'll laugh so hard, I can't help but join in. Soon, both of us are shivering and covered in wet leaves, pieces of weeds caught in our hair, our curls plastered to our faces.

Using the natural shower, I'll hold her hand and stand still, faces turned towards the sky. If it's raining hard enough, we'll be washed clean. If not, I'll use a cloth to brush the leaves from our skin, then wrap Aster in a blue beach towel Jack brought last year and take her inside, her wet head tucked under my chin, shivering against my chest.

I'll stand her up on a chair and rub her all over with the towel, until she stops shivering. Only when she is warm again, do I use the towel on myself. Then I'll dress us both in our finest clothes and wait for Jack.

Rain baths always make Aster happy. I hope it rains for her birthday, whichever day it is.

With the doll done and the paint drying, it looks at me from its perch on the table. A chill shivers down my back. I chalk it up to a memory of a cold rain bath with Aster. With its messed up eye, the doll looks like its winking. I would swear the eye does wink and I jump away from it. The doll topples sideways from its seated position on the table, its head crooked, its face staring at me.

Feeling foolish, I remind myself the eyes are painted on, not the kind that can open and close. Still, I don't like the doll staring at me.

I return it to its original hiding place under my bed.

Feeling unnerved, and knowing Grass will look after sleeping Aster for a bit, I step outside into the night.

After the heat of the day, the cooler evening air feels wonderful. There's just a bit of a breeze, enough to keep the worst of the mosquitoes away. My feet wander in a familiar direction, although it has been weeks since I have had a chance to sneak away from the cabin to my favorite hiding spot.

I follow the wandering of the creek to where it cuts into the ground, the sides of the banks rising above my shoulders on either side. Just a few yards more, and the small cave-like cut out in the bank looms like a dark hole. I think it's an abandoned muskrat hole that has half-collapsed, worn away by spring flood waters. I don't question why the hole is there, I just enjoy it.

I've never come here at night, and I suddenly wonder if an animal has also found the depression into the bank and made its home there.

"Hey," I call sharply into the opening. "If anything is in there, come out."

There is no sound from inside.

I drop to hands and knees and climb into the hole in the bank.

The walls of the small opening brush against my shoulders. Roots hang from the ceiling, brushing against my face. The sharp, deep scent of earth fills my nose. If I wrap tightly on my side, I can fit my entire body into the hole. Not caring that I'm getting dirty, I curl inside.

It's cool under the ground and my skin relishes in the lack of heat. If I turn my head just right, I can see the moonlight glittering on the creek.

I feel safe in the hole, surrounded by ground, unable to be touched. The earthen blanket comforts me, as I listen to the moving water and watch the moon cross the sky.

If I turn my head to the right, I can see a red

blinking light far through the trees.

The light is one of the reasons I come here. Its existence makes no sense to me in the world we live in now. Jack says electricity is destroyed along with society. The single red light slowly, silently flashes high in the sky.

A vague memory of the light at the grain elevator at the feed mill in Maddison flitters through my mind. Did that light somehow survive? Is the light I see now from the feed mill running on some sort of solar power?

A breeze moves the branches in the thick forest and the light disappears.

I look at the moon again, listening to the night. In the far distance I hear engines and what might be vehicles. Jack says those sounds are from military vehicles, the Maddison Militia, he calls it.

"Never go near the roads," he's warned many times. "The Maddison Militia patrols the streets now. You'd be a tasty treat for those evil men."

When I first came to the woods, the fear of the militia was enough to keep me to the cabin.

Only Jack could keep me safe. Only Jack protected me from the sick intentions of the wild men in the world outside our trees.

Thoughts of the world beyond make me shift deeper into my earthen cave, my safest place. I think of Aster safe in the cabin with Grass to protect her and I watch the moon glitter on the creek.

"Beautiful," I whisper. "Just beautiful."

My eyes droop and I fight against the drowsiness. "Maybe just a moment," I mutter, not wanting to return to the cabin, not wanting to return to the pressing responsibilities of running a home and caring for a child.

Here in the hole, nothing needs done.

Here in the hole, I'm free.

I allow my eyelids to close, shifting a little to fit more completely into the hole.

"Nellie, where the hell are you?!" My eyes fly open as Jack bellows through the darkness. The moon has barely moved, so I know I wasn't asleep for longer than a few moments.

"Nellie!"

His shout is followed with a series of angry

barks.

I claw and kick my way out of the hole, knocking dirt loose. Brushing off my nightgown as well as I can, I run in the direction of the cabin.

Jack wasn't supposed to come home, but now that he has he's angry.

Chapter 5

SHERIFF KINGSLEY

A knock on the interrogation room door interrupts the flow of her story. I'm so absorbed, it takes me a moment to return to the present.

"Come," I bark more harshly than necessary. The door opens and Deputy Dallmeyer enters with two cans of Pepsi and a Snickers bar.

"I brought this for you like you asked." He darts his eyes at Nellie and then to the table as if he's afraid to look at her. The young woman does have an other-worldly air about her, but Dallmeyer's reaction is over the top.

"Just set them down and go get her daughter," I snap. He sits the candy on the table but knocks both cans of Pepsi over. The unopened blue cans roll across the table. Nellie grabs one deftly.

Sensing his hesitation about her, she makes

a fake lunge at Dallmeyer and he flinches. A huge smile crosses her face. "I don't bite," she says to the slight deputy.

He rubs his thin mustache anxiously, a nervous way he has that always irritates me.

Have some self control, man.

With a power of will, I keep myself from sighing. "Is Deputy Paxton back from the scene yet?"

Dallmeyer whips his head away from surreptitiously staring at Nellie. "He just got here."

"Nellie, help yourself to a Pepsi and I'll be right back."

"I want Aster."

"I know," I hedge. "She's coming. Just sit tight for a moment, please. I'll bring her back with me."

Nellie crosses her blood stained arms across her chest and leans back in her chair. The bright blue cans of soda sit untouched. She's stonewalling me until she gets her daughter.

Shuffling Dallmeyer out of the room, I enter the hall. "Stop staring at her like that. You're even creeping me out." I tell him.

"It's like seeing a ghost." He looks over his shoulder at the closed door. "Do you think that's actually her?"

"I don't know for sure. We haven't gotten that far yet. Where's the girl?"

"She's with the Nicole and Maribeth Johansen right now. She won't let go of Johansen. The social services interviewer hasn't arrived yet."

A frizzle of excitement slithers into my belly at hearing Nicole is here. I expected that wherever Maribeth Johansen is involved, Nicole would be close by. I fight for professional calm. "Is Paxton with them?"

"Yeah he's watching them all. I put them in the conference room. Thought they'd be more comfortable there."

I'm surprised at Dallmeyer's thoughtfulness. He didn't do that because Nicole's here did he?

He doesn't suspect anything. There's nothing to suspect.

Stop lying to yourself.

I open the door and my eyes search for the

blond woman first. Nicole sits next to her sister, hovering and protective. She looks up as I enter and meets my eyes. The sizzle of reaction between us catches me off-guard with its intensity. She holds my eyes a moment. The investigation, the reason she's here, the entire night disappears. All I see is her blue eyes boring into mine. All I feel is the pull of my body towards hers.

The attraction we've felt at her sandwich shop is stronger here, intensified by the circumstances of the case.

"Sheriff Kingsley," she says. I drink in the sound of her voice.

"Nicole." I barely manage to keep a husky tone from my voice.

Maribeth Johansen doesn't miss the note.

A small girl clings to Maribeth, a wild mane of curls blocking her face. Maribeth pushes the girl's curls from her face and eyes me closely. She gives the tiniest of knowing nods. I remember with a flash that Maribeth used to be a detective in the major crimes unit in Fort Wayne and she doesn't miss much. I'll have to be more careful about hiding my feelings around her.

Or just be honest.

Deputy Paxton clears his throat and I'm drawn back to why I came into the room.

"Nellie wants to see Aster." I address Paxton, keeping my gaze away from Maribeth. Where her sister is everything light and sweet, Maribeth is dark and deep. She's been through things that would break a lesser human. Sometimes I'm not sure she didn't break and the face we see is just a mask.

Concerns about Nicole's sister will have to wait. Right now Nellie must be my focus.

Hearing her name, the tiny girl clings tighter to Maribeth, refusing to let go, even for her mother.

"Shh, baby girl," Maribeth soothes. "The Sheriff will not hurt you. Your mommy wants to see you. She needs you right now." I'm surprised at the loving tone she uses, then remember Maribeth once raised two children of her own.

Aster shakes her head, her curls bouncing

wildly. "Mama's all bloody. I'm scared."

"Your mama just wants to make sure you are okay. Will you come let her see you for just a moment? She has candy," I add.

Nicole shoots me a disapproving look, silently mouthing "Candy?"

I shrug helplessly.

Aster loosens her grip on Maribeth and turns to me. "I had candy once. I like candy." Her dark eyes are huge and haunted. "Can she come with me?" She squeezes Maribeth.

I force my face to smile, but inside I cringe. I may have feelings for her sister, but I've seen Maribeth at her lowest and it wasn't a good view. It's hard to reconcile that woman with the woman holding this child in front of me.

Maribeth doesn't wait for an answer, just carries Aster from the room. "Let's go." She calls over her shoulder. "Nellie wants her daughter."

"Don't mind her," Nicole says softly. "This whole thing has shaken her. Has us all pretty worked up."

"How's Ella and the others?" I ask about her

daughter. I want to pull her into my arms and tell her everything will be okay now. I want to touch her cheek, I want to run my fingers through her silky hair.

I need to tell her about my growing feelings first.

This is not the time or place.

Nicole touches my arm, the briefest brush of her fingers against my skin. The world spins for a moment.

"Ella and her friends are good. They're just excited about what happened. I sent them to the sandwich shop to get food for everyone. I hope that's okay."

If Deputy Paxton wasn't watching, I might just kiss this woman.

Instead, I straighten my spine. "That's perfectly okay. We'll get their full statements when they get back."

"How's it going with Nellie? Does she need anything?"

"She just wants her daughter." I suddenly remember I'm in the middle of a huge investigation and I can't stand here and flirt with Nicole all night no matter how much I want to.

"Thanks for being here," I say. Paxton or no Paxton, I squeeze her hand for the briefest of spectacular moments. Her smile gives me strength to return to the interrogation room.

Maribeth waits in the hall. Aster has released her tight grip and is looking around the Sheriff's Department with wonder.

"It's so bright," Aster says. "You have a lot of candles?"

Candles?

I open the door. Maribeth strides inside with confident steps.

"Thank God you have her," Nellie says to Maribeth. "Aster, baby, are you okay?"

Aster seems shy and nervous. "Uh-huh." She sticks a dirty finger into her mouth.

"Sheriff Kingsley brought us some treats. Do you want some candy?"

Aster lifts her head from Maribeth's shoulder. "Is it chocolate?"

Nellie looks at me for confirmation. I nod.

She takes the Snickers bar from the table

and hands it to Aster. The wrapper crinkles as Aster looks it over closely. Confusion scrunches across her face. Maribeth comes to her rescue, "You have to take the wrapper off first."

With the chocolate exposed, Aster takes a tentative taste. She smiles at her mother, "Better than berries."

We all laugh nervously.

"Now you see that Aster is fine and taken care of, can we continue?"

Nellie's face grows somber. "Can't I keep her here with me?"

"Do you really want her to hear all the details?"

Nellie shakes her head no. "Thank you for looking after her for me," she says to Maribeth. "Thank you for everything tonight."

Maribeth looks uncomfortable at the praise. "Just keep telling the Sheriff the truth and everything will be okay."

They lock eyes and some sort of wordless communication passes between them. I shift uncomfortably.

"Everything?"

"Everything that you can remember."

"What if I don't want to remember it all?" Nellie's voice sounds strained, like a child's whine, reminding me of her young age.

"Just do the best you can." Maribeth pats Nellie's shoulder. "Now give your mama a kiss, Aster." Aster kisses her on the cheek, leaving a smudge of chocolate behind.

Nellie seems to sink into the chair at the small touches. She makes no move to wipe the chocolate off her face. It mixes with the blood and mud stains already there.

Chapter 6

NELLIE

Jack wasn't supposed to come home, but now that he has he's angry. He's never come home this late and definitely never come home to find me gone. Small sticks stab my bare feet as I run through the woods towards the cabin. Brush pulls at my nightgown, slowing my progress as if the woods don't want me to return to him.

Jack's bellow rings through the night, demanding my return. I fool myself that he's more worried than angry at my absence.

Worry or anger, his agitation is palpable as I run to the front of the cabin where he waits in the yard. Grass is in the doorway, growling low in her throat.

"Where the hell have you been?" he demands turning on me but keeping an eye on the dog.

I brush at my nightgown and smooth my curls, saying lamely, "I went for a walk."

"What is this?" He swings a meaty arm in the direction of Grass. "Jesus, Nellie, I've only been gone half a day and this is what I come home to?"

"The dog just showed up this morning." I keep my head bowed in submission, the way I know he likes. "She's a nice dog."

"She's a nice dog," he repeats in a mocking sing-song. "She's growling at me like she owns the place."

"Grass, stop." My command does nothing to calm her. My agitation adds to hers. "Grass, sit."

With a whine in her chest, she obeys.

Aster suddenly appears, wrapping her arms around the dog's neck. "Look Da-da. I have a friend." She turns her sleepy face to her father, a mixture of hope and worry in her large eyes.

"A friend, huh?" Jack's anger melts a few degrees not that the immediate danger has passed.

I push the advantage, "You see she's a good

protector. She thought she was protecting us."

"From me? Dumb dog." Jack moves on, leaving the issue of Grass behind. "Get the bags. I had to fight hard today to find the things you need."

"Thank you, Jack. We owe everything to you," I say automatically, secretly breathing a sigh of relief at the change of topic.

Picking up the canvas bags lying in the grass, I gush, "These are so heavy. You found us so many things." I brush close to him, and say quietly so only he can hear, "You are so brave and so strong." I then kiss his cheek. The stubble there pricks my lips. The smell of his sweat pricks my nose.

He visibly relaxes and rubs a hand across his face, "It was a long day." He shoots a look at Aster and Grass in the doorway. "As long as the dog behaves, it can stay."

The words sound friendly enough, but I hear the unspoken threat in them. If Grass can't stay, I know how he'll get rid of her. I don't want to think what he'll do to the innocent dog.

With the bags weighing me down, I climb

the four creaking steps to the doorway. "Time for bed, Aster. You, too, Grass."

Sensing she won the quiet battle, Aster skips to her cot in the corner. Sensing the immediate threat has passed, Grass follows her small charge.

I light a candle and the cabin springs into a life of dancing shadows. The bags thud heavily on the wooden table. "Had to go all the way out to Pebble Road today." Jack says, suddenly behind me, his body too close. "Getting harder to find things now."

I want to ask why he came home early. I want to ask why he thought he'd be gone all night. I have a hundred questions that I don't ask. For the first few years I lived here, I used to beg for him to take me with him on his scavenging trips. "It would be faster with two of us," I'd explained. He told me it was too dangerous. Told me it was for my own good to stay here.

I yearned for people.

He told me the only people left were brutal and dangerous.

I yearned for anything besides these four walls.

He told me this cabin was the only safe place left for me.

I cried at night for a life I barely remembered.

He told me that life was gone, that world was destroyed.

All that remained for me was Jack and the things he brought home in the bags. Until Aster. Once I realized I was pregnant, leaving the cabin never crossed my mind again. I would do nothing to endanger her.

So I spend my days waiting for his returns.

A shiver or excitement flutters in my belly at the prospect of what the bags might contain. These bags are my only lifeline to the world beyond these trees.

Jack pulls out a chair and sits down heavily as I take the items out of the bags. He watches me with anticipation. The heaviest bag contains canned goods, baked beans, green beans, that sort of thing. The flutter of excitement in my belly fades. I'm not sure what I expected the bags to contain, and feel foolish for hoping for something that I know won't happen.

"Food, thank you. We were running low." I stack the canned goods on the table and give Jack a broad smile.

"Open the second bag," he says. "You'll like that one."

Against my will, excitement grows again, as I peek inside the bag. A scent of something floral and sweet wafts out.

"Perfume?" I ask.

He grins and nods, the candlelight transforming the smile into something hideous. "Doesn't it smell good?"

I pull out the glass bottle and give it a sniff. The floral scent is strong, not necessarily unpleasant but not pleasing either. I tell Jack what I know he wants to hear. "It's lovely. Thank you"

"Now you can smell good for a change."

I let the insult roll off me like water on a duck's back. If I let every little barb Jack says bother me, I'd been a blubbering mess years ago. I set the bottle of strong perfume as far away from me as I can without being obvious about it, then reach into the bag again.

There are a few shirts in the bag, silky things with flowers printed on them. The blouses are much too fragile and dainty for daily wear around the cabin and not the style Jack normally brings home for me to wear for him. The floral prints are pretty, but the words "old-lady-clothes" come to mind. "These are beautiful," I lie. "The fabric is so soft, and the buttons are so shiny." I struggle to find good things to say.

"I didn't think you'd like them, but I knew you'd like the flower pattern. You can use the fabric to make something else, right."

I try not to sigh in relief. I didn't want to offend him, but I didn't want to wear the blouses either.

"Look again, there's more."

Not even a flutter of excitement at looking again. There are only two things left in the bag, a black silky nightgown and a pair of high heeled shoes.

My stomach fills with dread at the items. This isn't the first time he's brought home similar items. Jack likes to dress me up.

His grin is huge now and it doesn't take the shadows from the candle to give it a sinister twist. He shifts in his chair, reaches for my leg, bare under my cotton nightgown. "That's a gift for both of us."

I try not to flinch away from his touch, but my leg moves against my will. I swat at an imaginary mosquito on my leg to cover the movement. "Thank you," I say quietly. "And thank you for the food."

There's a third bag to open, and I pull it closer across the table. Jack puts his hand on the handles, holding the bag closed. "This one's not for you."

Startled, I look him full in the face. He's rarely brought home things that he didn't allow me to see. "Why?" I ask before I can stop myself.

He leans closer, the candle illuminating his entire face now. In the light, I clearly see scratches on his cheek. Four long marks from just below his eye to his chin. Forgetting about the mystery bag, I ask "Jack, what happened?"

He looks confused.

"Your face is all scratched. Are you okay?"

He touches the marks with surprise, then takes the candle into the bedroom and looks at himself in the mirror over the dresser. I follow. He seems as startled by the scratches as I am.

"I had no idea sh-," he sees me in the reflection. "Shitty branches scratched me," he finishes.

"Let me put some antiseptic on those," I offer.

Jack shakes his head and brushes past me out of the bedroom. "Don't worry about it. They'll heal and be gone soon enough."

He places the candle back on the table and slides the straps of the mystery bag over his shoulder. "I'm going to the creek to clean up. Why don't you get changed." He nods to the black nightgown and shoes suggestively.

I pick up the silky fabric with trepidation. Across the room, Grass growls very low in her chest, her brown eyes glow in the light of the candle.

"That dog better not ruin our fun," Jack warns. Taking the bag with him, he leaves the cabin, tossing a, "Put on some of that perfume, too."

I obey, of course.

Not obeying rarely ever crosses my mind anymore. I focus on the good things, like the soft feel of the silky black fabric against my skin. I try to walk in the high heeled shoes, but I'm usually barefoot and the heels are a lot of work, not to mention they are too small. After a few stumbling steps, I get the hang of it. I walk around the cabin in the shoes, putting the canned goods away on the shelves near Aster's bed.

My daughter is sound asleep. Grass watches my every move with an intensity that unnerves me.

"He's not that bad," I whisper to the dog.

Her eyes continue staring at me. I feel the need to explain, to defend. "It's how I got Aster. Maybe I'll get lucky and have another baby."

I know another baby is a long shot. If it hasn't happened by now, it probably isn't going to happen. The thought of another child to love, of another human to share my life with is the only thing that gets me through the night with Jack.

Chapter 7

JACK

The day started out normal as coffee, but ended up exhilarating. A few scratches are worth the excitement that came by getting them. Stupid of me to let Nellie see them. She's growing too observant. Once they reach a certain age, they start to think too much.

I push thoughts of Nellie's maturity out of my mind. She's young enough still.

Its fifty four steps to the wood shed from the front of the cabin. Fifty four steps I can do in the dark. I spin the dial on the lock with ease, barely needing the moonlight to see the numbers. I open the shed and the familiar scent warms me. Wood, the slight remainder of blood and the lingering smell of fear. If the earlier events hadn't excited me, just being in the shed does.

The only thing besides memories in the shed is the metal cabinet where I keep all my treasures. Special finds that I hide from Nellie. It's not her business what I do while I'm out. Not her business what special trinkets I keep as mementos of special nights like tonight.

The heavy bag holds treasures beyond anything I have found before. I take them out one by one and place them in the cabinet. The slivers of moonlight seeping into the shed illuminate the many items I keep locked up. I add the new ones and run my fingers across the cool surfaces. My blood rushes as I touch them.

In the dim light, the picture of the girl, my girl smiles at me. I'd taken the picture on an especially wonderful day together. "A picnic," she'd suggested. My young brain, soaked in love, agreed. She'd smiled at me, and I'd done as she asked.

I always did as she asked, willingly, lovingly.

Until she asked to break up and my soul was crushed.

I had no control over her leaving, no choice in the shattering of my young heart.

I only had this picture of her smiling and blonde and eternally thirteen.

And a burning to recapture what I felt with her. Nellie helped soothe that burn.

Only thoughts of Nellie in the nightgown I acquired tonight can drag me away from my cabinet of secrets. Nellie would be disgusted if she knew who last wore the nightgown.

Nellie will do as she's told.

This pleases me as much as anything.

Chapter 8

NELLIE

Jack's chest hair prickles against my bare back. I wriggle further way, but he pulls me closer instead. Soon the morning heat causes sweat to form between our skin. The feeling of it slick and hot makes my stomach roil, I scrunch my eyes shut against the sensation.

He moans in his sleep and shifts, throwing his arm over my shoulders, wrapping me close. I pretend he holds me out of love, and in his way it is love. Love tinged with possession. His arm weighs heavy on my shoulders, effectively pinning me to the bed.

I shift uncomfortably, desperately hot, needing to get away from his body.

"Stay." Half command, half request.

"I need the outhouse," I say.

I feel him recoil in disgust. I shouldn't talk of such vulgar things. His arm remains over my shoulders.

I open my scrunched eyes. Now that I said it out loud, I really do need the outhouse. Both his hands are close to my face, hands I've seen a thousand times.

Today they are stained with red. The fingernail beds and under the nails are dark red. My first instinct is to clean them. We must be clean at all times. Then I remember he already went outside last night to wash up.

I look closer at the stains, recognize the color from when Jack brings home a squirrels that he make me gut and clean and cook for dinner. Free food.

Only one thing stains like that.

Blood.

I sit up, suddenly unable to be near those hands. The hands that he touched me with last night.

I wonder if he left blood on my skin.

"What are you doing?" he grumbles. "Lay back down." More demand, less request. I don't follow it.

Jack makes me sleep on the side of the bed

that pushes against the wall, so I'm forced to wriggle to the foot of the bed to get out. Some of the sheet pulls with me, exposing his chest. In the full daylight I can see more scratches on his chest. Freshly torn skin that had been pressed against mine just moments before. The scratches on his face are angry and red.

There was no bush.

He was in one hell of a fight.

"Why are you looking at me like that, did I grow two heads or something?" He laughs at his lame joke. I'd be less distressed if he had grown two heads. Better than the scratched and bloody remnants of some late night confrontation he's wearing.

I don't answer right away, just examine his wounds, trying to make sense of them. He always says how dangerous it is outside of our woods. He constantly warns me that the only safe place for Aster and me is here in the cabin. Did he have to fight for the food and clothes he brought home?

Is that why his hands are stained with blood? *Careful girl. Don't rattle him.*

"You're all scratched up. I'm worried about you."

He looks at his chest, rubbing at the scratches as if they will wipe away. "Damn braches."

The evenly spaced marks are not from a branch, and the blood under his nails is not from him.

I suddenly feel sick and confused and dirty. "I'm going outside for a moment. I'll be back to make your coffee."

Jack pulls on a t-shirt, covering the worst of his injuries, effectively wiping out their existence. With shaking fingers, I slip a shirt and shorts on, anxious to get away from him, anxious to go wash last night from my skin.

Aster is still sound asleep, but Grass lifts her head as I cross the cabin to the front door. I make a clucking sound with my tongue, and she bounds out of bed to follow me. The dog sniffs wildly as we make our way to the creek, her nose in every nook and cranny she can find. The running water of the creek beckons with the promise of cleanliness. Around a bend, hidden from the cabin, I find a deep spot and pull off my clothes. The water is only about knee high this time of year, but it is cool and refreshing. By dropping to my knees, I can wash all the important parts, splashing water on myself, searching for remnants of blood that Jack may have left on me. I

I scoop water in my hands, wishing I had remembered to bring the pail and wash cloth. I pour the scooped water over my shoulders and let it drip down my back. It causes goose bumps to pop up all over my skin.

Jack's scratches were deep and some looked freshly opened this morning. I imagine red streaks of his blood on my back where I can't see them or reach them. I could ask Aster later to wipe them away if they truly are there. She's so inquisitive now that she'll ask questions, questions I don't know how to answer.

Instead, I lower myself into the water and tip my head back. As soon as my ears fill with water, I begin to float. The current wants to pull me away, and I want to let it. Instead, I grab a branch and hold. I imagine the blood stains washing away with the moving water. I imagine my concern with where the scratches came from and how Jack's hand are so stained drifting away too. I've learned not to question, not to think.

Be thankful and move on.

Running my fingers through my floating curls with the hand not anchoring me to the branch, I wash out any cares. Aster is safe. I am safe. Nothing else matters.

"Mama?" I hear distantly through the water. "Grass?"

I pop my head up and holler to Aster. "We're over here, baby."

Soon her dark hair and wide eyes appear between the tall grasses at the edge of the creek. "You took a bath last night," she points out, her head tilted, her arm around Grass.

I stand, dripping and reach for my clothes. "And now I took a bath this morning."

Aster accepts the change in routine and moves on. "I'm hungry."

"You're in luck, Jack brought us some new food last night. We can have a feast."

"Jack left."

"He left already?"

Aster looks at the ground and shuffles her bare feet. "He yelled at me."

I pause in pulling my t-shirt on. "Why would he yell at you?" Concern and guilt fills me. I should have been there to protect her, not floating in the creek.

Aster looks at the wet spot on her nightgown. "Had accident last night and he got mad." She sticks her fingers in her mouth then takes them out again. "He said I was more trouble than I was worth." Tears well up in her dark brown eyes.

"Oh, baby. You're no trouble at all." I reach my open arms for her. "Come here and lets get you cleaned up."

Aster steps into the creek with her night gown on. I wash her and the gown. I make it a game, cause her to smile and forget her troubles. Inside, I'm seething. How dare he yell at her for something she can't control.

Clean and refreshed, we return to the cabin. Jack is gone.

Jack rarely leaves without saying good-bye, giving me instructions and letting me know when to expect him back. The last part always feels like a warning.

Sure enough, the canvas bags he takes on his scavenges are gone and so is he. The cabin feels lighter without him. I feel lighter after cleaning up in the creek. I feel impulsive and reckless and ready for adventure.

After breakfast, I grab our pails and ask Aster, "Want to go look for blackberries?"

She squeals with delight.

"It's getting late in the season, but we should still be able to find some."

"You'll love berries, Grass," she tells the dog. "Yummy."

I first cover us both with mud. The day is unusually calm and hot. The mud will protect us from both the bugs and from sunburn.

Happily swinging her pail, Aster asks, "Ready?"

She doesn't wait for my answer, just darts down a path we've found berries on before. Grass bounds after her.

"Don't get too far ahead," I yell into the trees.

It doesn't take long until I lose sight of Aster and Grass. I fight the tiny flutter of panic in my chest at losing sight of her. We've walked this way before lots of times, and I feel certain the dog won't let anything happen to her.

Apprehension only a mother can understand climbs into my heart.

In the distance, I hear the unmistakable howl of a coyote. The sound during the day surprises me. Normally we only here them at night. Normally the predators are farther away.

I stop in the woods, the trees stretching out in every direction as far as I can see. I strain to hear her, but the only sounds that reach my ears are the birds chirping in the trees and a squirrel letting me know exactly what he thinks of intrusion.

And the coyotes baying.

"Aster?" I call.

The squirrel chastises louder. I turn in a slow circle, no longer sure what direction she went.

"Grass?" I try the dog, sure she doesn't know her ridiculous name yet. "Here doggy, want a treat?"

The woods grow quiet. The squirrel has given up and the birds have stopped singing.

A breeze creaks through the branches and the rattling leaves sound like applause.

A vehicle passes by somewhere, closer than usual.

Images of the Maddison Militia finding Aster and stealing her from me flood my mind.

"Aster?" I scream into the woods. A coyote answers me, and my feet begin running in the that direction. I pound through the brush, dropping the pail, berry hunting forgotten.

We've gone too far from the cabin. Jack warned us to stay close. Tells us nearly every day that the cabin is the only safe place.

Why didn't I listen closer?

I dart through the woods, turning here and there, screaming for my daughter. My lungs burn for air and I'm forced to stop, hands on my knees, gasping. Over the sound of my ragged breathing, I hear a whistle.

One note, long and steady.

Aster can't whistle.

Instinctively, I drop to the ground, hiding.

"Pepper?"

A male voice nearby, too close.

Terrified, I crawl under a nearby bush, wondering desperately where Aster is.

"Lord, please let her be safe. Don't let that man find her," I whisper into the ground close to my face.

The man whistles again, calls out for Pepper. He's closer this time. I try to make myself smaller, to disappear under the bush and into the ground. I yearn for my hole at the creek, needing the security of surrounding earth.

Footsteps crashing through brush grow closer. My heart pounds wildly.

Jack told me what men do to women they find alone. Images of what the man will do when he finds me floods my mind, panic overrides my senses. I shove my hand against my mouth to keep it from screaming in fear.

The footsteps grow even closer. "Pepper,

here girl." Followed by another long whistle.

The man is only a few yards away now. I open my eyes a tiny sliver and I can see his boots. The need to run, the urge to flee screams in my mind.

He hasn't seen you. Stay still.

Aster is out here somewhere.

Thoughts of Aster keep me in place. If the man doesn't know I'm here, he doesn't know Aster is out here either.

The thought calms my strung out nerves, but the sensation only lasts a moment.

From behind me, a crashing comes through the brush, followed by barking.

Grass explodes from the woods, running straight for the man.

I expect Grass to growl, to bite, to protect us. I expect the man to run in terror.

He exclaims in relief, "Pepper, there you are."

Through the branches of the bush that hides me, I watch as dog and man reunite. The mystery of where Grass came from is solved. Grass puts her paws on the man's chest and licks his face. I finally look past his boots to his face.

I'd expected a grizzled, burly man, someone to be afraid of.

The man is younger than I thought he'd be, about my age. His blond hair falls messily on his forehead and even from under my bush, I can tell his eyes are a bright and clear blue. He doesn't look terrifying. He's so delighted to find his dog, his face glows.

I drink in every detail. He's the only person besides Jack and Aster I have seen for years. A deep yearning replaces my fear. A need for companionship drowns out Jack's warnings that all strangers are dangerous.

This man doesn't appear dangerous. Someone who loves his dog so much he's out here looking for her can't be as bad as Jack says everyone is.

I shift under my bush, preparing to make my presence known, when Aster runs towards the man.

"My dog. Give her back." Aster throws her tiny body at the stranger, pounds his thighs with her fists.

The man steps away, startled, doing his best to fend off his small attacker.

"What in the world?" he says shocked by her sudden appearance. "Where did you come from?"

Aster doesn't answer. "Come Grass. Go home." She puts her arm around the dog's neck and pulls.

"Wait, little girl, that's my dog." He touches Aster's arm.

Already half way out from the bush, I spring into action. "Don't touch her!"

This time the blond man's mouth falls open in surprise. "Look, I'm not trying to hurt her, but this is my dog."

I step between Aster and the man, pushing her behind my legs. Grass goes with her.

"The dog came to us. She's ours now." I lift my chin and meet his dazzling blue eyes. "If you want her back, you'll have to fight me for her."

Chapter 9

NELLIE

The young man puts his hands in the air and backs ups a few steps. Some of the tension leaves my shoulders. I would fight to the death for Aster if needed, but I'm glad he didn't push it.

"Who are you guys?" he asks. His tone is soothing and calm, so unlike Jack's.

"Who are you?" I counter.

"My name is Eli. This is my aunt's dog, Pepper," he motions to the dog.

"Her name is Grass," Aster argues, poking her head around my leg. "She's mine."

Eli lets that pass. "What are you two doing way out here?" He looks us over closely. I'm suddenly conscious of the fact that we are both covered in mud and must look ridiculous to him. I push my hand through my blond curls and my fingers catch on a leaf stuck there.

"My name is Nellie, this is my daughter Aster."

Eli's blue eyes grow so wide, I can see the whites all the way around them. "Daughter?"

My shoulders stiffen. "That's what I said."

"Where do you guys live?"

I know better than to fall for that. "Where do *you* live?"

Eli points in the opposite direction of our cabin. "My house is over on Turner Rd."

The information means nothing to me, but I like listening to his voice. "Where's that?"

"About a mile or so that way. Pepper disappeared yesterday morning and I've been out looking for her. I finally thought maybe she'd come to these woods and gotten lost." He looks at the dog. "Turns out I was right."

"This is private property. You're not allowed to be here." I'm not even sure private property is a thing that exists anymore, but I need him to go away.

Eli looks at the ground, "I know. I'm sorry. I didn't know anyone lived way back here."

I panic, not wanting him to know about the

cabin. "Who says we live here?"

He shrugs. "I just assumed."

He raises his eyes and meets mine. I want to pull away from his gaze, but something about him draws me in. We stand there for a long moment, stuck together like magnets.

"Mama, you said we could find berries," Aster interrupts the heavy moment. "Grass is coming," she challenges.

Eli looks from the dog, to Aster, then back at me, clearly confused on what to do.

"Let the dog decide," I say.

"Pepper is my dog," he protests. "Plus, she has a vet appointment tomorrow."

I blink in confusion. The expression sounds familiar, but it has no meaning in the current state of the world. "Who takes a dog to a vet now? I'm surprised you even have a pet."

Eli's face scrunches, "Why wouldn't we have a pet? Most people do." He looks me over more closely. "Are you two okay?"

I lift my chin again, "Why wouldn't we be okay? We have plenty of food. Besides, Jack will be back soon." I make it sound like a threat in case he gets any ideas of following us or worse, stops being so nice.

My words upset him, but I don't understand why. He runs a hand through his blond hair and it flops back on his forehead again.

Aster is pulling on my hand, wanting berries. Grass is at her side, her decision between Aster and Eli made.

"She chose me," Aster says. "Now go away."

"Aster, manners." I chastise.

Eli takes a step towards us. "Nellie, I don't understand. You can't just take my dog."

"Are you going to tell the Militia on us? Are you going to attack a woman and her child? You don't seem like that kind of man."

His mouth falls open like he wants to say something but no words come out.

"Don't follow us. I told you I'd fight you if I have to, and Jack is much stronger than I am."

He takes another step towards us. "What are you talking about? I'm not going to fight you. And what is this about the militia? There's no militia. Do you mean the police?"

"Nice try. There are no more police." A strange stirring begins in my stomach. He seems so sure of himself.

"Can I call someone for you?" He takes a small, flat box out of his pocket. "Do you need help? Something isn't right here."

"Berries, Mama." Aster is agitated by my growing concern and pulls on the hem of my shorts, tugging me to follow. She and Grass then run into the woods.

I look towards her retreating back then meet Eli's eyes again. "I'm sorry about your dog, but Grass chose Aster and Aster doesn't have much."

"Nellie?" he raises his hand and touches my shoulder. Through the coating of mud, his warm fingers make my skin tingle. "What's going on here?"

I lean into his touch for a glorious moment and the world falls away. The destroyed world doesn't matter, the fight over who the dog belongs to doesn't matter. What Jack would do to this man if he knew he was here doesn't matter. All that matters is his hand on my shoulder.

He drops his hand and the world comes back into focus.

"Forget you saw us, Eli. Pretend you didn't find your dog. If you are any kind of decent man, do not tell anyone we are here. It's the only way to keep us safe."

"Safe from what?"

I back away from him, and raise my arm as if to encompass the world. "Safe from the world out there. Safe from the strangers that want to steal from us and hurt us. Safe from everything."

"That's not how the world is, Nellie."

Aster calls for me. I turn towards her and walk into the woods without another word.

I don't want to believe Eli.

Confused and scared of the thoughts forming in my mind, I break into a sprint. I push past branches and brush. Hidden sticks and poking rocks stab at my bare feet, but I keep running. I catch up to Aster and Grass. "Run with me," I call.

Aster laughs and her short legs pump to

keep up. Grass runs with us, her pink tongue lolling from the side of her mouth.

The three of us are free and happy, once again alone in the woods.

I wake late in the night to an empty bed. Jack hasn't come home. I lay in the moonlight and think about Eli and all that he said. Through the window, I watch the moon slide across the sky. I'm wide awake and full of thoughts. Anxious and unable to lie still, I climb from the bed. After a quick check on Aster, her arms tight around Grass, I slip into the night.

I need my hole, need the earth to swallow me. I find it easily and climb inside. I search for the blinking red light on the grain elevator. I thought the light was a fluke, a left over from the world before.

Was I wrong?

I listen to the sounds of vehicles passing far beyond the woods. The Maddison Militia on patrol. Eli said there was no Militia. Did he lie to me?

Did Jack lie?

"I have to take Pepper to the vet tomorrow."

Such a normal thing to say and said with such conviction.

Snippets of life before seep into my confused mind. A brown fluffy dog I once had as a pet, a trip to the vet to get its shots.

My mother smiling at me.

I push that thought away with all the will power I can muster. I learned years ago that thinking of my mother only leads to pain.

Her face flashes into my mind uninvited. Her curls are like mine, her eyes are brown like Aster's. Tears burn my eyes. I don't want to think of her. She's been dead for years along with the rest of my family.

"I saved your life," Jack has told me over and over. "If it wasn't for me, you'd be dead like they are."

The blinking red light grows blurry through my tears. Sobs choke my throat. I turn away from the light and face the dirt wall of the hole. The smell of earth fills my nose and the ground drowns out my sobs.

The face of my mother is replaced by the face of Eli.

"Lord, help me see the truth," I beg. "I'm so confused. Please help me."

I cry until I can't cry anymore, then I climb from my earthen hiding spot. I take my time returning to the cabin. I'd seen the cabin as a safe haven before, as a home. In the dark, barely visible in the pale moonlight, the door, open to let in the cooler night air, looks like a menacing mouth, waiting to gobble me up.

Grass appears at the doorway, a darker shadow inside the mouth.

I want to keep walking. I want to go anywhere other than here, no matter the danger.

But Aster is inside.

I pat Grass on the head as I enter the cabin. She climbs back into the cot with Aster.

My empty bed offers no relief to my tired mind. I feel empty and lonely. Eli's deep blue eyes fill my mind making the empty feeling inside larger.

I climb onto the floor and reach under the

bed for Aster's doll. I once again have to reach far into the corner for it. I grip the pink dress and pull the doll out.

Taking the doll to bed with me, I curl on my side and hold it to my chest like a child. The short hair smells vaguely of burned plastic, but I don't care. Wrapped tightly around the doll, I cry myself to sleep.

Chapter 10

SHERIFF KINGSLEY

Maribeth takes Aster and the chocolate back out the door. We are alone in the room, the quiet deafening. I crack open a Pepsi, and hand Nellie a fizzing can. "Would you like some?"

She takes a cautious sip, then wipes at her nose. "It tickles." She takes another big sip then sighs. "I haven't had a can of soda in so long."

"Did Jack bring you sodas?"

Nellie looks at me seriously, shaking her head slowly. "I remember them from before."

Now we're getting somewhere.

"Nellie, does the name Jolene Starkman mean anything to you?"

She goes completely still. The fizzing of the soda in the can is the only sound in the room.

"Jolene is dead."

"How do you mean, dead?"

"Jack killed her and created me."

"Are you Jolene Starkman?"

"Not anymore."

"Nellie, how did you come to live with Jack?"

"He saved my life. When the world changed and everyone died, he saved me. He told me I was special, that he loved me so much he couldn't let anything happen to me."

"Do you remember the night he saved you?"

She takes another sip and nods.

"For a long time I forced myself to forget it. Forced myself to forget everything from before that night."

"And now? Do you remember?"

Another sip and another nod.

"Do you want to tell me about it?"

"I don't want to, but I will."

"Let's start with something easy, how did you first meet Jack?"

Nellie's face scrunches for a moment, a fleeting expression of pain. "I've always known him. He'd been friends with my parents. He had come to cook-outs and parties. He was just always around. He even came to my sixth grade graduation. He gave me a new Xbox as a gift."

She laughs nervously. "Mom was mad. Said it was too extravagant a gift for a little girl."

"What did you think?"

"I wanted the game." She shrugs and takes a sip of the Pepsi. "I didn't think it mattered."

"Did he often bring you gifts?"

She picks at a mud caked fingernail. "Sometimes. New clothes, jewelry, that sort of thing. I hid them from my parents."

"Why did you hide the gifts?"

"He said they wouldn't understand. I said I got the clothes from a friend at school. The best thing he ever gave me was a cell phone." She gets a dreamy look on her face then gives her head a shake. "I can't believe I forgot all this. Mom and Dad said I wasn't old enough for my own phone, but Jack bought me one anyway. I definitely hid that from them. He'd call me every morning to wish me a good day. He'd send me links to articles about riots and bad things in the news. I didn't care about that stuff, but he'd always ask if I read them, so I did. It wasn't that much to ask in order to have a phone. I liked having it. I felt special. Of course, my friends had the number too, although only a few of them had their own phones."

The obvious signs of grooming her make my stomach roil. Jack knew what he was doing. I get the sinking suspicion Jolene Starkman, Nellie, was not the first girl he groomed.

"Do you still have the phone?"

She shakes her head slowly. "Jack said it burned in the fire."

I'd seen what was left of her house, and understand why we never found a phone we didn't know she had.

"Do you want to tell me about the fire?"

Her shoulders stiffen and she crosses her arms over her chest, rubs her upper arms as if she's cold. "I suppose I have to."

"You don't have to do anything you don't want to do."

"Don't I?" she asks cryptically. "I don't

want to be here, but I am."

I steer her back on track, "Tell me about the fire, Nellie."

She shivers and rubs her arms again. Then she sits up straight in the chair, her hands spread on the table top for support.

"I used to have nightmares about it. Jack told me they were only nightmares, that it never happened. I don't understand why I forgot it until now."

"Sometimes the brain does what it must to survive. You were in total survival mode."

She slides her hand across the top of the table, pushing the fallen mud pieces into a neat pile.

"I woke up choking," she starts. Her voice wavers, but grows stronger as she speaks. "My room was full of smoke. At first, I had no idea what was going on, I only knew I couldn't breathe. My door was open just a crack and in the crack I could see red and orange flickering. I didn't think fire at first, I thought maybe a TV was on in the hall or something. Stupid, I know."

"Was the smoke alarm going off?"

"No. It was quiet except for the crackling of the fire in the hall. That's why I didn't know what it was. I'd always been taught the alarm would go off. When mom burned something in the kitchen the alarm would go off."

"So you wake, up. What happened after that?"

"I got out of bed and went to my door. I couldn't breathe, kept coughing. I pulled my door open and looked in the hall. That's when I panicked. The hall was full of flames."

She scatters the mud pieces across the table and reaches for her Pepsi. It's empty so I hand her the other one. She takes a huge gulp.

"Were you able to go down the hall?"

She shakes her head so strongly more mud joins the pieces on the table. "I couldn't go down the hall. Flames were pouring out of my parents' bedroom door. I remember thinking that was odd because they always kept their door shut, but it was open. I tried to go down the hall to the stairs to get out, but it was too hot. So I went back to my room and closed the door behind me. That's when I saw Jack."

"Where did you see him, outside?"

"No, he was in my room. He'd climbed through the window. My window looks over the garage roof. He told me to climb out onto the roof and we could get to safety. I was so scared, I just followed him. I trusted him. We got onto the garage and then he slid to the ground. At the edge he told me to slide off and he would catch me. I was so frightened. I looked over my shoulder towards my bedroom window. The flames had reached my room. I had nowhere else to go. I lay on my belly and slid over the edge. Jack caught me. I remember his hands on me, keeping me from falling to the ground."

She stops talking and stares at the wall behind me.

"That's the last clear memory I have of my life before," she continues.

"Did he drug you?"

Her arms wrap around her again. "I suppose so, but I didn't realize it at the time. I just know that for the last several years, if I think about my past, it always started with the cabin. I only ever lived in the cabin. My name was Nellie. I had lived there with Jack for always. Jack was my whole world." Her face burns red and she looks towards the floor. "You must think I'm an idiot to have forgotten who I was, to have believed him."

"I think you went through something terrible and did what you had to survive. No one is judging you here."

She raises her head slowly and meets my eyes. "Can I ask you a question?"

"You can ask me anything."

"Are my parents really dead like Jack always told me?"

I wish I could tell her something different. "They died in the fire," I say gently.

She looks away. "He killed them to get me, didn't he?"

"We think so."

"Did you look for me? Did you try to find me or what?"

"At first we thought you were burned in the fire, too. It took several days until we realized you were not there. We checked out Jack as part of the investigation, since he was a family friend. He was clean as far as we could tell. His girlfriend said he'd been home all night in bed next to her. The cabin property belongs to his great uncle in Florida. We had no idea to look there for you."

"He had a girlfriend?" Her voice is a mix of disbelief and a touch of jealous anger. "A girlfriend at home and he stole me?"

"They broke up soon after."

"Probably because he was spending every night with me." She's unusually defensive. She runs a hand through her curls, but her fingers get caught in the tangles and mud. "I'm getting tired. Do we have to keep doing this?"

"I'm sorry, but we do. We need to understand what happened tonight."

"If I can't have Aster with me, can I at least have the doll?"

The childish request reminds me she's barely more than a child herself, mother or not. She was clinging to the doll when we found her. The singed and melted thing sits on my desk at the moment.

I take pity on the girl. "I don't see what it could hurt. I'll be right back."

I know I sat the nasty doll on my desk earlier, after I'd coerced Nellie to let go of it. The doll is not on top of my desk now. It sits on my chair, winking at me with the painted on eye.

Hating to touch the thing, with a special hatred of dolls due to a previous case, I pluck it up by the dress hem with two fingers. The doll feels heavier than expected and seems to wiggle. I drop it on the tile floor. It stares up at me with disapproval.

Rubbing my hand down my face, I say out loud, "Get a grip, man." I'm loathe to touch the thing, so slide it along the floor with the toe of my boot. Once outside the interrogation room, I'm forced to pick it up again. This time it is light as a hollow plastic doll should be.

Once again using only two fingers, I pick up the thing, then take it to Nellie. She cradles it against her as she might Aster. "There she is. Deputy Kingsley, meet Elyse."

I flinch at the name. "Elyse? Why in the world did you name her that?"

Nellie looks at the doll with adoration. "I don't know. Aster said the doll told her that was her name."

I swallow hard. If I never hear the name Elyse again, that will be too soon.

"You said before it all started with this doll. I don't understand what that means."

Nellie turns away from looking at the doll and says, "Jack hated this doll. It made him mean.

Chapter 11

NELLIE

I awake to the doll being ripped from my arms. Here it clattering across the floor.

"What are you doing with this? Loving on it?" His voice hisses near my ear, almost unrecognizable in his anger.

I instinctively reach for the doll, try to protect it, but it lays in the far corner of the room, upside down against the wall, one leg indignantly hanging down. "I was just sleeping."

"Pretending this doll was a man?" The venom confuses me.

"No. I was thinking of-." I almost say my mother, but memories of beatings after mentioning my mother years ago stop me. "I was thinking how nice it would be to have another child."

Jack laughs loud and long at that. "You

don't need another child. Aster is enough trouble." His anger has abated a little, a tide receding but threatening to return.

"I know. I'm sorry." I apologize as contritely as possible. "I just miss you when you're gone." I play the game he loves, the game that keeps me safe. "My heart misses you when you are out working so hard providing for us." I keep my eyes down, submissive and appearing broken. The words and the act that have been so easy in the years past burn against my will now.

The game works its magic and Jack's anger disappears. He reaches out and musses my curls. He even picks the doll up off the floor and hands her to me. I sit the doll against the pillow and climb out of bed. I seal the game and wrap my arms around his waist and hold him close. He seems surprised by the uninvited show of affection.

"You did miss me," he says, crushing me to his chest so hard I can barely breathe.

"Always." I wriggle to be let go. "Are you hungry?" The night is just beginning to fade into morning, the cabin shrouded in pale light. "Maybe some coffee?" I leave the confining bedroom and start building a fire in the stove.

Jack yawns loudly. "Coffee would be good. I've been up all night." He doesn't keep his voice low like I did and soon Aster stirs in her cot in the storage corner. Grass climbs out of the bed and comes to stand between Jack and me. The hair on her neck is raised a little and she watches him with weary eyes. I pat the dog on the head to calm her before she starts something. If she wants to live with us, she needs to learn to accept Jack the way we do.

"I see the dog's still here," Jack says.

"Aster loves her."

"Da-da!" Aster's excited voice rings through the cabin. I hold still, hoping Jack will give her attention this morning. To my surprise, he takes her in his arms and holds her close. Aster beams at the attention. Grass tenses under my calming hand.

"Looks like someone else missed you, too." I say, happy to play the game. As I prepare Jack's coffee I wonder why everything feels like make believe today. Why my family feels like a farce.

"Did you play in the dirt, Da-Da?" Aster asks, inspecting Jacks hands.

I freeze in the act of putting the coffee pot on the wood stove. The heat of the fire flickers against my skin, matches the tension suddenly filling the room. I can feel Jack's eyes burning into my back, daring me to turn around and look.

I don't turn around, pretend I didn't hear the question.

My mind burns with questions. How dirty must he be if Aster noticed?

He doesn't answer the question, just puts Aster down and walks out of the cabin.

I watch through the window until he reaches the creek, then call Aster close. "Why did you ask him that?" I whisper.

She holds up her hand, "Dirty nails. Da-Da hates dirty nails."

I flick my eyes out the window. Jack is bent over the creek, furiously scrubbing his hands. Self-consciously, I check my own nails then check Aster as well. We are both scrubbed clean. Even the night time visit to my dirt hole doesn't show.

"Don't ask him about it again. Da-Da works hard when he's not here. He gets dirty sometimes."

Aster has lost interest in the dirty nails, but nods anyway. She takes Grass outside into the early morning. "Don't go far," I call out the open door. Jack suddenly appears in the doorway.

"That girl of yours is getting nosey," he says. "I liked her better when she didn't talk so much."

I don't like the undercurrent in his voice.

"She's just a girl." I fight to keep my eyes off his hands, wish I had seen what Aster had seen before it was washed away. "She's not even three yet."

"Yes she is," he says cryptically.

His mouth is smiling, but it doesn't reach his eyes.

I scrunch my face in question.

"Today's her birthday. It's why I came

home early." Something in his tone rings with untruth, but I play along.

"Today? I knew it was getting close, but the days all kind of blend together." A surge of excitement courses through me. "I don't have anything ready." I flutter to the cabinet. "I need to make a cake and wrap the doll."

Jack suddenly puts his hands on my shoulders and turns me around. "I already took care of everything. I got lucky and found a cake and a stuffed bunny for her last night."

I let him turn me around. "You found a cake?" I look around the cabin. The bags he takes on his scavenging sit in the corner. Two of them have objects in them.

He nods eagerly. "It was in the back seat of someone's car. I knew Aster would love it, so I took it."

Stole it.

I push that thought away. Jack says scavenging is the only way to get things now, that money has no value. The memory of Eli flickers, but I push that away too.

It's Aster's birthday. That's all that matters

at the moment.

After checking to be sure Aster and Grass are still outside, I pick up the bags and set them on the table. One of them clinks heavily against the wood tabletop. "This one isn't for you two." Jack takes the heavier bag away and sits it by the door.

I'm too excited about the prospect of cake to wonder about the mysterious bag. I peek inside and see a plastic box. I look at Jack in disbelief, then pull the cake out. It is the most beautiful confection I've ever seen. Fluffy white frosting topped with delicate pink icing flowers.

"Jack, it's beautiful," I gush, tears stinging my eyes. "It's too pretty to eat."

"I'm sure we will manage to take a bite," he teases, his good mood returned. "You really like it?"

I pull the cake out of the bag, "I love it. I'm sure Aster will love it too. She's never had a cake like this."

I set the plastic encased cake on the rough wooden counter. It looks alien there, the shiny plastic gleaming in the morning light.

"Don't forget the bunny," Jack takes the stuffed rabbit from the bag. The gray bunny is obviously new. Its fur is spotless and a tag hangs from its ear. The oversized eyes stare at me, daring me to question its presence in my cabin.

"It's adorable. She'll love it." I suddenly remember the doll I found and prepared for her. The doll is garbage compared to the big eyed bunny. "But what about the doll?"

"You keep the doll." The words are hard. "You seem to like it."

"Maybe she can get both gifts," I mutter. I know which one she'll like better.

It's not a competition.

"Cake for breakfast," Jack says with a yawn. "Then I'm going to bed. It's been a long night."

"Just let me wrap this in something before we call her in." I find the flower printed blouses that Jack brought home last time and wrap the gray bunny in the floral fabric. I tie the arms of the shirt into a bow. I have to admit the result is pretty.

Taking the other blouse into the bedroom I go for the doll I left sitting against the pillows. I stand staring at the unmade bed, no doll in sight. "Jack, we left the doll here, right?"

"I guess," he answers. I hear his boots dropping to the floor as he takes them off. He then joins me in the bedroom in his socks. "She was right there," he points to the pillow, then lifts a blanket. "Here she is. Guess she was playing hide and seek." He tosses the doll to me and I catch it awkwardly. She feels heavy, solid. I lose my grip and drop her back on the bed. Her pink dress rides up showing her belly.

Jack looks at the doll with disgust. "You sure you want to give that thing to Aster?"

I feel a rush of protectiveness and hurry to straighten her dress, cover her plastic skin. "I like her. She's a fighter." I cradle the doll against me carefully, run my hand tenderly across her shorn hair. "She went through a lot to get to us."

"If you like her that much." He shrugs.

"Wrap her up and let's do this." He yawns again.

I use another blouse to wrap the doll and set the pretty floral gift next to the other, next to the precious cake.

Only when everything is ready do I call for Aster.

Chapter 12

NELLIE

Aster tumbles into the cabin with Grass close on her heels. The cake and gifts are set up on the table and she stops short when she sees them.

She turns her wide dark eyes to me in question, her mouth open in a dark "Oh" of surprise.

"Happy Birthday, baby girl." I beam at my daughter, filled with emotion at her reaction.

"My birthday?" She approaches the cake and gifts with wonder. "I'm three, right?"

"Right, three years old."

She reaches a hand towards the cake, a tentative finger lingering over the icing.

Jack makes a sound of denial, and Aster pulls her hand away guiltily. "Let's wash up and then Nellie can cut the cake for you."

Aster sticks the offending finger into her

mouth, then hurries to the wash basin.

I wash my hands, too and make her giggle while pouring water on her hands. "Didn't know it was my birthday," she whispers.

"We wanted to surprise you." I tell her.

I don't have cake candles, but put one of our regular candles among the pink frosting flowers. It looks grimy and offensive on the lovely cake, but it's the best I have. I sing to her. Jack mumbles along, stifling a yawn. She seems delighted at the attention.

"Blow out the candle and make a wish," I prompt at the end of the song.

Aster closes her eyes tight and says, "I wish that man never comes to take Grass again."

My blood turns to ice as she blows out the candle.

"What man?" Jack demands.

I send Jack a pleading look. "Let's just have some cake and open presents." He isn't falling for it. "Please. I'll tell you everything after we do this," I add in a low whisper.

Jack just glares as Aster says, "I get presents, too?"

116

"Cake first," I say, hoping against hope that Jack will stay calm and not ruin Aster's birthday.

I cut her a large piece and one for Jack, then one for me. When I first saw the cake, I couldn't wait to taste it, to sink my mouth around the fluffy frosting. A memory of previous cakes, before the cabin flash through my mind. I have no room to think about that, I'm consumed with Jack's barely contained anger. It radiates off of him like the heat from the stove.

Aster either doesn't notice or is so used to his foul moods, she doesn't care. She eats her cake with delight, even shares a few bits with the dog.

I nibble one bite, then leave the rest untouched, fear at the upcoming conversation making my stomach ache.

As she licks frosting off her fingers, Aster asks for presents. I hand her my doll gift first. She unties the arms of the blouse and the doll slides out. Aster flinches as it lands on her lap.

She picks up the doll gingerly and looks it

over. "It's a tiny mommy."

"It's a doll," Jack grumbles.

"Yellow hair like Mommy." She rubs the short blond tufts remaining on the doll's head. Aster looks at me for approval. I grin like a maniac to reassure her.

"What do you want to name her?" I ask.

Aster scrunches her face for a moment, closes her eyes. "Her name is Elyse," she says.

I'm surprised at the choice. Since Aster doesn't know anyone besides Jack and me, she doesn't know any names to choose from. As far as I know, Elyse is a word she's never heard before.

"Why Elyse?" Jack asks, shifting uncomfortably in his chair.

"That's what she said her name is." Aster shrugs. She then purposefully lays the doll on the table and slides the second gift towards her.

The stuffed bunny with the over-sized eyes is received with squeals of delight. Immediately, Aster makes the bunny hop across the table then onto Grass's back. "Her name is Hoppy."

A much more suitable name than Elyse.

Aster climbs down from her chair, Hoppy gripped tightly in her fist. "Tell Da-Da thank you for the bunny and for the cake," I say.

Aster hops the bunny over to Jack and makes the bunny kiss his cheek. "Thank you Da-Da. I love Hoppy and the cake."

Elyse lays forgotten on the table. I try not to take it personally. Of the two gifts, the bunny is definitely better. I just put a lot of work into making the doll presentable. Maybe Jack was right and I should have thrown it back when I first found it in the creek.

"Why don't you take Hoppy and the dog outside and go play," Jack says. His tone is forced casual, but I hear the storm brewing. As soon as Aster is out of ear-shot, he turns on me with full fury. "What man came to take the dog?"

"No one came," I hedge. "We were out picking berries and he was out looking for his missing dog. We just ran into him."

"You let him see you? You talked to him? Haven't I trained you better?" The questions come one after the other, spittle flying with is agitation.

"It wasn't my fault. He was just there. Then he tried to take Grass away. Said she had a vet appointment."

I throw that last sentence like an accusation.

"No one goes to the vet anymore," Jack says coldly. "He lied to steal the dog."

Jack is the one lying. I let him think I believe him, more game playing to stay safe.

"That's what I told him. I said to leave us alone and never come back or the Militia would haul him away." Not exactly the words I used but I want to see Jack's reaction.

"The Militia would take him if they found him out in the woods without the proper paperwork."

"Eli says there is no Militia."

The words hang in the air between us.

Jack's face clouds over. "Eli says?" He takes a step closer. "You know his name?"

I stand my ground. "He told me his name. I just remembered it. He's the only person besides you and Aster I have seen for years."

I want to make my mouth stop talking. I want to look at the floor and beg Jack to forgive me for running into the stranger. I want my life to stay safe and boring and the same.

Something deep in me wants a different life.

"Eli made it sound like the world hasn't fallen into chaos and ruin like you have said. He made it sound like the world was still normal."

Jack's nostrils flare in anger.

Alarm bells in my brain tell me to stop talking. My mouth doesn't listen.

"Is the world the same? Where do you go every day? Do you really scavenge things or do you just buy them from stores?"

Jack takes a slow step closer. My mind is screaming for me to shut up, but I keep talking. "You didn't find this cake in the back seat of an abandoned car. And the bunny is brand new. It has a tag on its ear still."

"What do you know of the world out there? I'm the one fighting and clawing for everything you have here. If you must know, I stole the cake and the bunny from a store that had closed down and is abandoned."

I want to believe him, I want play the game.

In a voice just above a whisper, I say, "The cake is fresh. You just bought it."

The slap across my face surprises me. "Don't pretend you know anything beyond these four walls," he hisses.

I touch my stinging cheek in surprise. Finally my mouth has nothing else to say, only hangs open in shock.

He grabs me by the hair and pulls my face so close to his, I can smell frosting on his breath. "I'll teach you to doubt me."

Thank God Aster is out in the woods somewhere with Grass and Hoppy, because I'd hate for her to see Jack drag me out of the cabin and into the trees. Every time I fight back he twists his hand tighter in my hair and slaps me again.

We stumble through the trees to a part of the woods I never go.

The wood shed.

Since my first day in the cabin, Jack said never to go to the wood shed. It was his private space, strictly off limits.

I can't imagine why he's dragging me there now.

Chapter 13

NELLIE

The woodshed looms in the trees a dark square of planks and a sagging roof. The door is shut tight, a metal lock hanging from the door. The metal glints in the morning light.

Why does it need a lock? We don't even close the doors of the cabin, let alone lock them.

He stops at the door and stands me on my feet. He has to let go of my hair to turn the dial on the lock. I crane my neck to see the combination he puts in, but he spins the dial too quickly for me to catch more than the first number.

My feet want to run, but I know that will only mean another slap or worse.

"What are you going to do?" I squeak out.

The face that turns to me is barely

recognizable as Jack's. "Keep you from entertaining any more men."

"I didn't entertain him. I told you we ran into him while picking berries"

He opens his arms wide, "I don't see any berries. You lie."

"Ast - I ate them all." I don't want to say Aster's name. In his current state, its better Jack doesn't remember she exists, focuses his anger on me.

"You ate them all. How convenient." In a practiced motion, he takes the lock off the door.

"What else did Eli tell you?" He makes the young man's name sound like a curse word.

"He didn't tell me anything. I told him to forget he ever saw us and to never come back."

"Sure you did. You probably invited him over. You were probably thinking about him when I found you wrapped around the doll this morning."

I feel my face grow warm. I had been thinking about Eli when I fell asleep with the doll.

Jack notices the pink blush and flies into a rage.

"I knew it!" He grabs my hair again before I can react. "You slut. I should have known better than to trust you."

The punch to my gut knocks the air out of me and my head swims with pain. Jack rips the woodshed door open and tosses me unceremoniously onto the planked floor. "You are all the same. I give you everything and you only take."

I lay in a heap on the floor of the small building. Jack kneels beside me, leans close to my face. "I trusted you." His eyes are full of pain and fury, his voice full of betrayal. "I loved you."

"You can still trust me," I plead, desperate to play the game, to soothe him. "I love you with all I have. You are the only thing in my world."

For a brief moment, Jack's face softens and I think I won. Then he pulls away from me.

"I wish I could believe you. Mark my words, things are going to change around here now."

Before I can scramble off the floor, the door shuts. I throw my body against it, but hear the lock click.

"Let me out! I'll do anything you want. I love you so much, please don't leave me here."

The planks of the walls have small gaps between them. I push my eye to a gap and watch in horror as Jack disappears into the trees.

I shake the handle of the door, throw my shoulder against it. Pain radiates through my arm, but the door doesn't budge. I check the gap again, but Jack is gone.

Then I think of Aster.

Will he hurt her? Will he leave us again? Who will take care of her?

I listen to the woods, yearning to hear her voice, to hear the dog, to hear any sign that she's okay. She knows as well as I do to avoid this part of the woods. The woodshed is off limits.

The rough wood planks scrape my bare knees as I drop to the floor. "Lord, please watch over Aster. Keep her safe until I can be with her again. Let Jack realize his mistake and release me from this cage."

I am not practiced in prayer, but I add an amen and hope for the best.

Climbing off the floor, I test every inch of the shed to find a loose board or a way out. As dilapidated as the shed looks from the outside, it is surprisingly sturdy. One board is slightly loose and I tear at it until my fingernails are worn and ragged.

The board holds.

With no escape immediately apparent, I sit on the floor and wait.

Although Jack calls it the wood shed, there isn't any wood stored inside. The room is empty except a cabinet in one corner. The cabinet is metal and has a lock on it as well. The red dial stands out against the black metal, a bright spot in the dimness of the shed. As I wait, I stare at that lock, wondering why he has a locked cabinet inside a locked shed.

Wondering why he locked me inside and what he plans to do.

Will he leave me here until I starve to death?

Will he come back, and what then?

Can I convince him to forgive me?

Instead of listening to the questions pounding through my head, I focus on the cabinet. Maybe there's something inside that will help me escape.

The sun has risen high and the heat in the shed is growing unbearable. Sweat drips down the sides of my face, into the scrape on my left cheek where he hit me. My right eye is beginning to swell. I ignore the pain. My hands are damp as I pull on the lock on the cabinet door. The lock slips out of my wet fingers. I wipe my hands on the nightgown I haven't had a chance to change out of and try the lock again. It's like the one on the door, a combination lock with a spinning dial. I try every combination of numbers I can think of. Snippets of a metal locker and a similar lock dance through my head.

This time I don't push the memories away. A sequence of number jumps into my head, 21-27-31, my old locker combination. I try the numbers, sure it will open the lock.

The lock stubbornly remains closed, the red dial mocking me.

I try the numbers again, desperate and not knowing what else to do. The lock refuses to open.

Defeated, I slide down the wall between the metal cabinet and the wall of the shed. There's just enough room to hide here, to feel safe in the space. I huddle here as the shafts of sun from the gaps in the planks travel across the floor.

I lean my head against the wall as the heat bakes me into a stupor. My head spins and my bladder begins to protest the hours I've been locked inside. I shift into a more comfortable position, placing my palm against the wall, and my beaten cheek against my palm.

Under my fingertips, I feel a something scratched into the wood.

I lift my spinning head and inspect the plank.

Four letters are carved into the wood.

ANNA.

Chapter 14

JACK

Betrayal burns like acid in my stomach and my hands ache. I'm so tired of all of it. Exhausted to the core. I return to the cabin with sore hands and a sore heart.

She met another man.

The sting of it penetrates my heart.

Aster is in the cabin, playing with the horrid doll. "Where's mama?"

I don't bother with answering. The thing is too young to understand.

She watches me with her unusually big eyes that look like mine. "Can I have cake?"

"Take whatever you want. You will anyway."

I slam the bedroom door and fall face down on the bed. I've been up for 30 some hours, I need rest. The pillows smell like Nellie and a tiny surge of sympathy flames to life. I squash it with all my will.

She met a man.

All women are the same.

I wake later to an empty cabin. Aster and the damn dog are gone. So is a large portion of the cake. The whiny thing ate it. I drag my finger through the frosting and lick it off.

They're both becoming more trouble than their worth.

The box on the shelf beckons. I open the wooden lid and look inside at the yellowing bones. I pick one up and cradle it in my palm. A sense of peace, of completeness, overcomes me.

The idea blossoms in my mind. It worked before.

I close my hand on the bone and thank it for the guidance.

Get rid of them and start anew. It worked before.

And I know just who to talk to get the ball rolling. They've been after me for several months now for the thing. If the price is right, now is the time.

I gently return the finger bone back to the box and close the lid. I straighten the priceless box on the shelf where it has stood for years. A treasure I found when I visited my great uncle here as a child. The lovely wooden box has been displayed with pride ever since. The bones inside have been at times my friends and my instructor. My best ideas have come from them.

This is one of my best ideas.

After another finger-full of frosting, I head down the path to my waiting truck. It's a long walk, but I can't risk Nellie seeing the truck. I've trained her well. She rarely leaves sight of the cabin, let alone walks down the path this far to see the black Chevy hiding I the trees.

I start the truck and blast the AC. Living in the heat is one thing I wish I had planned better for. Maybe I'll surprise Nellie with a generator and I can solve that problem.

I turn on the radio and blast country music as I pull down the lane to the back road that borders the woods. A small red car passes.

The terrifying Maddison Militia.

I smile at the joke. I can't believe she's fallen for that one all these years.

I chose well when I chose her.

Chapter 15

NELLIE

When I read the name Anna scratched into the wood, a scream breaks from my cracked lips.

I scramble to my feet, desperate to get away from the name. My screams echo around the shed. A single thought echoes around my mind.

Someone else has been locked in here before. Locked in long enough to carve her name into the wall.

Terrified, I pound on the door, pound on every plank.

"I need to get out. Good God, please let me out." I pray again.

Aster.

Thinking of my daughter calms my terror enough that I can think straight. Maybe Aster can help. But how?

I'm not sure if she can help, but I need to see her, need to know she's okay. I've been in here for hours. She's been alone for hours.

Or with an angry Jack.

"Aster!" I yell as loudly as possible. "Aster where are you?"

I listen hard for an answer. The woods are quiet, my yelling scared any birds or squirrels into silence.

"Aster," I yell again, my voice growing hysterical.

He wouldn't hurt her would he?

I shove my eye hard against a gap in the wood, searching frantically for any sign of Aster or Grass in the woods. I see nothing but trees. In despair and fear, I slide to the floor.

Then I call for the dog, hoping her keen hearing will pick up my voice. "Grass, here girl."

Nothing.

Of course, she probably doesn't know her

name is Grass, she's only been with us a few days. What did Eli call her? Pepper.

"Pepper! Here Pepper."

I wipe sweat from my stinging face and try again. A faint bark carries through the trees.

A surge of excitement sends me to my feet. I call the dog again, sure Aster will follow.

The responding bark is closer this time.

Soon, the black form of the dog crashes through the brush towards the shed. "Good girl," I sob. "Good dog. Now where's Aster?"

I hear her before I see her. "The child takes a dog, the child takes a dog, hi-ho the dairy-o the child takes a dog." I have no idea where she learned the nursery song, sure I didn't teach it to her. The odd song coming from her tiny mouth startles me.

More importantly, the sound of her brings a rush of relief.

She's okay.

"Aster, baby. I need your help."

She stops several yards from the wood shed. "Why are you in the wood shed?"

I don't know how to answer the question

without scaring her. My eyes drink her in, checking every detail of her tiny body. She looks fine, not hurt or bruised or scared.

Pink and white frosting is smeared across her mouth. Apparently she got into the cake while I've been gone. I don't care if she ate the entire thing, I'm so relieved to see her whole and safe.

"Can you come a little closer? I need your help. I accidentally got stuck in here."

She slowly approaches the shed, and I notice the doll tucked under her arm. The bright pink of her dress matching the pink frosting on Aster's lips.

"Elyse told me to find you," she says.

"That's a nice doll to help me. Can you help me?"

She walks closer, nodding her head so hard her curls bounce wildly.

"Is there a lock on the door?" Aster probably doesn't know what a lock is. "Something shiny?"

She nods again and sticks her finger in her mouth.

I had half hoped the door was just latched, not locked, and Aster could open it.

"Is Jack in the cabin?"

Even through the small gap, I can see her tense up. "Yes." She takes a tiny step away from me. "He's sleeping."

Locked me up, then went to bed?

Now that I know Aster is safe, my body makes its discomfort known. My mouth is dry from hours in the stifling heat, my stomach rumbles. I can live with the hunger, but the heat and lack of water is making me light-headed.

"Do you think you can bring me some water? I'm very thirsty."

Aster seems excited to be able to help in the strange situation. "I can." She sits the doll against the shed wall before she goes. "Elyse wants to stay with you."

Without another word, Aster runs off in the direction of the cabin. "Grass, go with her. Protect her."

The dog doesn't need my prompting, she follows Aster everywhere.

While I wait for Aster, I sit against the wall trying to plan how I'll get the water into the shed. The gaps in the wood are not large enough to pass a cup through. There are gaps between the bottom of the planks and the floor. I kick at one and it breaks open wider, wide enough to pass a cup through.

I kick some more, hoping to break the board loose so I can escape. Another small piece of wood falls away, but the plank holds.

I imagine Anna had tried the same tactics and failed like I did.

How long had she been locked in here if she carved her name in the wall?

A scurrying sound behind me makes me freeze. It's too soon for Aster to have returned. I peak through the gap, but don't see anything outside that could make the sound.

I hear the sound again, turn in the direction it's coming from.

Through the gap in the wall and the floor, I can see the doll leaning against the shed. Sweat drips into my eyes as I watch the doll move to the right.

I wipe at the sweat, sure I'm hallucinating from the heat and dehydration. When I look back, the doll is gone.

Laying flat on the floor, I look out the gap where the doll had sat only moments before. I see tiny plastic legs walking a few steps, then stopping, as if she felt me watching and froze.

Hallucination. Only a hallucination.

I shove away from the view, move to the far side of the shed, putting as much distance between me and the doll as I can.

I won't hurt you. I want to help.

The words are in my head, only in my head.

I fight panic, fight the hysterical laughter that wants to escape my chest, fight the thought that I'm losing my mind.

I need water.

I scrunch my eyes shut and whisper to the air, "Aster, please hurry."

When I open my eyes again, the doll has returned to where Aster left her sitting against the wall of the shed.

Without taking my eyes from the hem of the pink dress that shows in the gap, I wait for my daughter to return.

The doll doesn't move again.

Aster soon returns with a cup of water.

"I'm here," she says proudly. "I bring water."

"Good girl, Aster." I gush. Can you bring it over here and slide it through the hole?"

Aster does as I ask. The red plastic cup may have started out as full, but it now only holds an inch or two of water. I slide it into the shed and drink it greedily.

The wetness calms my parched tongue, but ignites a need for more.

Should I send her for another cup or just wait for Jack to release me? He has to come back at some point. He can't leave me in here forever.

He left Anna in here.

Aster has sat in the dirt on the opposite side of the wall from me. She's picked up the doll and cradles it in her arms. I'm not sure I like her playing with it now that I've seen it walking on its own.

Or did I? Am I going crazy?

"What's Jack doing? Is he still sleeping?" I ask to distract myself from thoughts of my sanity.

"He left."

The two words pierce my heart.

"He left? Do you mean he went down to the creek or for a walk?" I ask desperately.

"He was gone when I got water."

"You sure he wasn't in the outhouse?"

Aster giggles. I take that as a no, but hope that she's wrong.

We sit for a long time as the sun lines through the gaps continue their slow march across the floor. My stomach grumbles and my mouth is dry as dirt. My bladder aches and I worry I won't be able to hold it much longer.

Aster sings quietly, leaning against the wall. She continues with the Farmer in the Dell and I find myself singing along with her. I'm not sure how I know the song, let alone how Aster knows it. Finally my curiosity gets the better of me.

"Baby, who taught you that song? Was it Jack?"

"I just learned it. You like it?"

"I love to hear you sing, but how did you learn it?"

"Elyse taught me."

The shed spins around me as I bake in the heat. Now I know I'm hallucinating.

I lose the battle with my bladder and have to squat in a corner of the shed.

Aster keeps singing, her voice growing loud and boisterous.

Weak and exhausted, I lay on the floor, the rough wood prickling against my face. I listen to my daughter sing and wonder if this is how I'll die.

As I fade into unconsciousness, I hear Aster say, "Look, Elyse can dance."

I don't want to look. I don't want to believe.

I just want Aster and I to escape to safety.

If safety even exists in the world anymore.

Chapter 16

NELLIE

I don't think I was unconscious for too long when I hear Aster exclaim, "Da-Da!" Her excitement at seeing her father even though he is the one that locked me in here breaks my heart. "Are you going to let Mama out?"

"You in there Nellie?" he asks roughly.

I want to snap, 'where else would I be?' but I wisely bite the bitter retort back. "Please let me out. I miss you." I hope the game will appease him.

The sound of metal rattling lets me know he's undoing the lock. "It's time for dinner. I'm hungry."

No apology, no explanation.

On hands and knees I scramble out of the shed, thankful to be released no matter what the reason.

Once free, I climb to my feet and wobble

towards the cabin. "I'll get something going right away." I straighten my back and lift my chin. Taking Aster's hand, the one not holding onto Elyse, with Grass on our heels, we walk through the gathering dusk towards the only home I know.

Back in the cabin, Jack acts as if nothing has happened, like it's any other evening. He sits at the table watching me prepare dinner. I first drink a glass of water, careful to down it slowly. I don't want to give him the satisfaction of seeing how thirsty I am.

I manage to put some sort of food together and Aster helps me set the table. The remains of her birthday cake are on the counter. A lot of the cake is still there, but nearly all the frosting has been eaten. Tiny tracks of fingers show in what remains.

Aster looks at the cake and then at me, worried she'll be in trouble.

I'm just glad she ate something while being alone all day.

We eat dinner in silence, a solemn end to a horrible day. My face aches from the beating

Jack gave me earlier and my body is still weak from the heat and lack of water or food all day. I just want to eat and drink and go to bed.

"I have to leave tomorrow," Jack says as if it's a change in his usual pattern. He leaves nearly every day.

"Oh?" I ask, feigning interest that I no longer feel.

"I'll be bringing a couple home with me. They want to meet Aster."

The words lay heavy in the room. Never in all the years I've been in this cabin with Jack has he brought someone home. I swallow hard against the lump suddenly choking me. He said the words calmly, but after his stunt today, I no longer trust him at all.

"See me?" Aster asks. "Why?" Bless her heart, she sounds so excited at the prospect of company.

I stare at Jack's face, searching for any clue to his intentions.

"They like little girls and I told them I had the best little girl in the world."

The words are simple enough, but my

stomach clenches with dread.

Aster bounces in her seat with excitement. "Best girl in the world," she repeats.

She's not wrong. She is the best little girl, but why do some strangers care about that?

Despite my fears about what the visitors might mean, I do my best to continue the game to keep the peace with Jack that night. In the morning I wake up with his arm thrown over my shoulders, a subconscious move to keep me in place. I wriggle against the weight, then climb out of bed.

"Are you going to be good today? Or do I need to lock the cabin?" I freeze in the bedroom door.

"You know you can trust me." I say as sweetly as possible.

"Can I?" He sits up in bed, leans against pillows. The scratches on his bare chest are red, angry streaks on the white of his skin.

I give him the biggest smile I can muster. The action makes my bruised face hurt. "Yes, you can."

Jack suddenly remembers the scratches on his chest and quickly pulls a t-shirt over his head.

I don't want him to think I was looking at them. "I'll make coffee," I say to distract.

I'm busy making coffee so I don't see the offense until Jack bellows into the cabin.

"What the hell is she doing up here?"

I turn slowly, half expecting a blow, to see what has set him off.

Elyse is sitting on his precious box.

I stare at the doll's melted face, dumbfounded.

"I-I have no idea."

"Aster!" He yells, waking my girl. She rubs her face and blinks at us from her cot. "Why did you put your doll here? You know my box is off limits."

"Didn't do it," she says sleepily. She darts her eyes from me to Elyse and back to me in confusion. Aster has never lied to me, and she's telling the truth now.

Elyse dancing yesterday.

"Well, the ugly thing didn't climb up here herself," he points out. It's a logical conclusion, but nothing with the doll has been logical.

Aster looks panicked now. She didn't ask me about the bruises on my face, but she's a smart girl and probably put the story together. Sensing her distress, Grass growls low and quiet.

"Aster can't reach that high," I point out, desperate to protect her from his wrath. I hurry across the room and take Elyse off the box before Jack can get his hands on her. The doll has been through enough. I search my brain for a plausible reason the doll is there and find nothing that makes sense.

My immediate thought is to appease Jack, to make him happy.

"Maybe I did it this morning." I add a huge yawn for emphasis. "I'm so tired and she was on the floor. I think I might have sat her on the shelf instead of the table in my sleepy state." I make my words sleepy and vague and add another yawn.

My fake yawning causes Aster to yawn in response. If the situation wasn't so dire, it would make me smile.

Jack doesn't seem to believe my story, but he has no choice except to accept it. How else would the doll get on the shelf? Grass didn't put it there.

Grumbling about lying wenches that he can't trust, Jack goes outside to the outhouse.

I hurry to Aster with the doll. "Hide this under the covers," I whisper.

"I didn't do it, Mama."

"I know, baby. I know."

"Elyse likes the box. She asks me about it all the time."

Aster looks so earnest it breaks my heart. She wants a friend so badly she's invented one.

"You tell Elyse to stay away from there."

I hear Jack on the back steps and hurry to finish his coffee. The sooner he leaves, the better.

After he's had his coffee and put on his boots, he takes the canvas bags and heads out. He stops at the open door and looks me straight in the face. "Don't make me regret not locking the doors."

"I won't. I promise. You can trust me."

"I'll be back this evening. I want this place spotless for my friends."

"It will be."

Without another word Jack slams the door behind him. I don't hear the metal sound of a lock or anything else that will keep us in. I stare at the closed door for a moment, the red checked curtain on the window swaying gently from the shock of being slammed. I hurry to the window and watch as Jack disappears down the path that leads to the world, the world I haven't seen in years, the world I'm starting to wonder might be different than what Jack has told me.

I open the door wide, letting in the morning cool and turn my attention to my daughter. "We're going to have visitors tonight." I try to force excitement into my voice even though I'm actually full of dread. "Want to help me clean the cabin to get ready?"

Chapter 17

ELI

I watch the mud covered young woman and her tiny daughter disappear into the woods with my dog. Once they are gone, I begin to question my sanity.

Did that really just happen?

The woman looks about my age, but she has a little girl, so she must be older. I'm sure I would have remembered seeing her at school. Maybe she's home schooled? Maybe she's part of one of those off-grid prepper families. Would explain her talk about a militia. Preppers have some pretty wild ideas.

My aunt won't be happy that I'm not coming home with Pepper. As I walk back to the four wheeled utility vehicle that carried me most of the way into the woods, I decide not to tell her that I found Pepper at all. That little girl needs her more than my aunt does. I'm fond of the dog, too, but it's a sacrifice I'm willing to make. It's obvious the pair don't have much. They were caked in mud, for heaven's sake.

I park the ATV in the barn and go to my aunt's back door.

My back door.

The newness of my new living arrangements still jars me. I realize my parents felt they didn't have a choice in sending me to this backwoods small town. Shoplifting isn't the major crime they made it out to me. A little pot never hurt anyone either. For heaven's sake, its legal in some states.

That argument hadn't worked on them. "Some time in the country will help you out," Mom had said. Dad hadn't liked it, but as usual, he refused to stand up to her.

Off to Aunt Liza's I went. In her back door I walk now.

"Did you find her?" she asks as I hang the ATV keys on the hook by the back door.

"No." I hate to lie. A stab of guilt mixes with wanting to protect Nellie and her daughter.

"Where did that dog get to? I was sure you'd find her in those woods. They go on and on, a perfect place for a high energy dog like Pepper to get lost in. I'd never go into them, they creep me out."

I fill a glass with water at the kitchen sink to avoid answering. After I gulp down the entire glass, I earnestly say. "I'm sorry."

"Oh, Eli, it's not your fault. That dog has a mind of her own. She'll come home when she's ready."

I doubt it, but don't contradict her. I stare out the back window at the woods behind her farm, the woods that stretch on and on. "Aunt Liza, does anyone live back there?"

She humphs in amusement. "In those woods? No way. You don't know the old stories from around here yet, but those woods are cursed."

She has my attention now. "Cursed how?"

"Well, not right behind here, but further down and way at the end of them is where a serial killer left a dead girl last winter. So that's not good. Even before that, bad things happen. Years ago a man killed his entire family, including his cow and his dog and his cat." Liza shivers at the memory. "Was a nasty business."

My mouth falls open in disbelief. "His entire family? When was this?"

"Oh, decades ago, now. But this town remembers."

"And that happened in those woods?"

"More or less. Like I said they go on and on, this was way down by Stickmiller Rd. but still." She lowers her voice. "I know it's crazy, but sometimes I swear I see lights dancing in the woods back there."

A shiver climbs up my back.

"A lot of people think the woods are haunted."

"Do you?"

She rubs her upper arms. "A lot of strange things happen around this town. I try not to think about it."

Not exactly an answer.

Are the mud caked woman and her daughter ghosts? I mentally shake myself. Aunt Liza might not give a definite answer, but I don't believe in that kind of thing.

Pepper is real and she went with them. That's enough proof for me.

In the weeks I've been living with Aunt Liza, Pepper has shared my bed. I feel lonely without her now. Images of the blond woman with piercing blue eyes dance through my mind as I toss under the covers. If I lay on my side, I can see the woods behind the house. As I watch, small dots of light move through the trees.

I sit upright and lean towards the window to get a better look. The woods are dark, the way they have always been. Aunt Liza's stories must be getting to me. Deciding to ask my friends at school about it tomorrow, I turn my back on the window and the woods and finally fall asleep.

Maddison High School is a lot different than the school I went to in Indianapolis, at least on the outside. My school back home was huge.

There were so many kids in each grade, you didn't really get to know everyone. It just wasn't possible. The entire building was state of the art and nearly new. The football stadium was spectacular, the science classes all had high tech labs, the cafeteria had several lines and options to choose from. More like a restaurant than a school cafeteria.

Maddison High was dingy and tiny in comparison. It suited me just fine.

I had a few friends at my old school, but no one I truly clicked with.

Here, I've already made a group of friends I feel I belong with. Our cafeteria may be smaller, but the friendships of my eating companions is huge.

Faye, the other new girl at the school waves me over after I get my tray.

"I thought we'd sit by the window today," she says as I put my tray down. Soon Noah and Ella join us. The three of them had already formed an unusually strong bond before I came to school. In the two weeks I've been here, they've taken me into their group.

We always sit alone. Sometimes I feel the other kids watching us, talking about us. I chalk it up to me and Faye being new kids, but sometimes I wonder. Noah and Ella have gone here all their lives, now they are outcasts of sorts. It's a mystery I plan to work on later. Today I have other things on my mind.

Once the four of us are settled and eating, I broach the subject. "Do you guys know anything about the woods behind my aunt's house being haunted?" I ask bluntly.

Ella freezes, her fork halfway to her mouth. "Why?" she asks breathlessly.

Noah pats her shoulder and the fork continues its journey to her mouth.

"My aunt told me last night that some horrible things have happened in the woods. She said strange things happen in this town a lot. Like a serial killer and some guy who killed his whole family years ago."

My three friends stare at me. I get the feeling they are sizing me up, testing me with their eyes. I must have passed the test.

"That serial killer situation happened on my

Aunt Maribeth's property. So did the man who killed his family."

"Holy shit," I mutter in surprise. Leaning forward, I say, "So it's true?"

Now Faye pipes in. "Do you believe in ghosts or demons or the supernatural?"

I begin to feel uncomfortable. "I never did before, but you guys are starting to scare me."

"Believe it, man. This town in cursed," Noah says.

Three sets of earnest eyes stare at me, daring me to doubt them. Remembering the lights I saw in the woods last night, my resolve slips. "Cursed?"

"Well maybe not the entire town, but certain parts of it," Faye says, shifting uncomfortably in her seat. "Places like my farm. It was haunted by a ghost named Elyse. She loved dolls."

The three of them look at their plates. "Was? Past tense?"

"We took care of it." Noah says in a tone that says the matter is closed. I sense a whole lot more to the story, but now isn't the time to get into it.

"Why are you asking us about this now?" Ella asks.

I debate whether I should tell them about Nellie and the girl. She begged me to keep her secret. I feel a sense of loyalty to her. "Just something my aunt was talking about last night."

"It doesn't have anything to do with the missing woman does it?" Noah asks.

"What missing woman?"

Ella leans close, excited now that we've moved away from talking of the woods. "Some woman was robbed last night and now she's missing. An older woman, Tonya something."

"I haven't heard that yet. And she lives here in Maddison?"

"Told you," Noah says. "Cursed."

Faye smacks him on the arm. "Stop that. I don't like that word."

Noah mumbles an apology.

"Do they have any idea what happened to her?" I ask.

The three of them shrug in unison. "You

gonna eat that?" Noah asks Ella motioning to the cookie on her tray.

"Keep your hands off," Ella says with a laugh. "You guys going to the football game tonight?" The subject officially changed, the moment to tell them about Nellie has slipped away.

I may not have told my friends about her, but Nellie is never far from my mind. By the next morning, I can't take it anymore. I need to see her again. I need to prove to myself she's real. I need to make sure she's okay.

Snagging the keys to the ATV off the hook by the back door, I holler to my aunt, "I'm going to tool around on the Rhino for a while."

I drive to where I met her the first time, then park the Rhino. "Nellie?" I call into the woods. I have little hope that she'd be near here. The woods are too thick to drive through, so I continue on foot in the direction they ran before.

Chapter 18

NELLIE

Aster and I spend the morning cleaning the cabin from top to bottom. Hoppy the bunny and Elyse the doll watch us from her cot. Once in a while Aster goes to the toys and whispers something in Elyse's ear. Then she smiles as if she's being answered. After yesterday's hallucination about the doll and finding the doll on the box this morning, Aster's attachment to her bothers me a little. But I have other things on my mind today. What do these people want with my daughter?

"Can we have berries for lunch?" Aster asks.

"We need to stay close to the cabin today," I say. Aster's face falls.

The cabin is clean and there's nothing left to do but wait with trepidation for Jack and his friends.

"Please. You can make cookies for Da-Da's friends."

I'm surprised at her attempt at manipulation. But if she wants berries that badly, I hate to disappoint her.

With the berry basket in my hand and Elyse in Aster's hand, we head into the woods with Grass. I know better this time than to stray very far. I don't need a repeat of last time. First almost losing Aster, then running into Eli.

Eli.

The young man has been on my mind despite everything else going on. Secretly, I hope we do see him. Secretly, I hope he told someone about us. Secretly, I wonder if it's safe for Aster and I to stay with Jack. Maybe it would be better if we tried surviving in the world on our own. At least no one would lock me in a wood shed.

Or would they? I have no way of knowing.

We don't make it too far into the woods before I hear crashing through the brush in the distance. As if summoned by my thoughts of him, Eli appears.

I freeze and grab Aster by the shoulder. Before I can stop her Grass runs towards the young man.

"Don't let him take Grass."

"He won't. I don't think he wants to hurt us. I think he wants to help us."

"Don't need help." She wraps one arm around Elyse and holds her tight to her chest. When we reach Eli she wraps her other arm around the dog, a not too subtle show of possession.

"I hoped that I would run into you again," Eli says. He brushes his heavy bangs off his forehead and they fall back into place. Even on only our second meeting, the movement seems familiar, comforting. My reaction to the young man surprises me.

Aster makes a humph of disapproval.

"She's afraid you're going to take the dog."

"I think Pepper wants to stay with you."

"Grass." Aster says emphatically. "Her name is Grass."

I can't help but giggle at her sassy attitude. But I feel it's my duty to correct her. "Aster, be nice. I told you Eli won't hurt us." I look at the young man with the question in my eyes.

"I'm not here to hurt you. I just can't stop worrying about you. Looks like I was right to worry." He stares at my face pointedly.

I touch my tender cheek with my fingertips knowing there's a bruise on one cheek and a black eye on the other side. I don't want to talk about it, so I don't. "Did you just come out here to look for us?"

"Yes." He says simply

"Even after I told you not to? I told you to forget about us and to not tell anyone."

"I haven't told anyone about you." The way he says it leaves a "yet" in the air.

"What is there to tell? We live in the woods, so what?"

Eli's back tenses. "Did you know there's a woman missing?"

"What does that have to do with us?"

"Probably nothing. Her house was robbed and she disappeared two nights ago." He looks at the ground, kicks his tennis shoe against the dirt. "Then I meet you to out here in the woods. It just gets me thinking."

"Thinking can be dangerous." I don't like the way this conversation is going. The news of a missing woman startles me. Two nights ago. Two nights ago Jack came home with the scratches on him. Scratches and blood.

"My aunt says these woods are haunted." He looks around at the trees as if an apparition might appear at any moment. "Says some crazy stuff has gone down not far from here."

"Crazy how?" I know the woods aren't haunted, or at least I would have said so before the mess with Elyse this morning.

"A serial killer left a body here last winter. Of course, it was a few miles that way, but the woods reach all the way there. My aunt told me to stay out of here."

"You should listen to your aunt. These woods are private." Aster says the words, but the tone and expression don't look like my daughter.

He takes a step back, startled by her gruff manner.

"I'm not trying to intrude, I just got worried."

In the same far away tone, Aster says, "We are not your concern."

She has Elyse up high on her shoulder as if the doll is talking into her ear. That combined with the rude attitude bothers me. "Aster, be nice."

I pull Elyse from her and the doll dangles from my hand by one arm.

Aster seems to return to her normal self. She looks a bit dazed and turns her big eyes to Eli. In a voice that sounds like hers, she asks, "You don't want Grass, what do you want?"

She asked the question I couldn't put into words.

Eli locks eyes with mine. "Maybe I just wanted to see you again." He holds my eyes for a moment longer than necessary. Aster starts singing the Farmer in the Dell under her breath.

"I remember that song from when I was a kid," Eli says, trying to win Aster over. "I like your doll." He's only being nice. Elyse has half her face melted off. The paint I used to draw on a new eye is already peeling.

I hand the doll back as she says, "Her name is Elyse. I got her for my birthday yesterday."

Eli seems to pale at the word Elyse. "My friends knew an Elyse and she liked dolls too."

"Your friends?"

"Some kids I go to school with Ella, Noah, and Faye. They had a run in with - well it's hard to explain." Aster holds Elyse tight to her chest. "You can't have my doll, either"

Eli laughs gently, "I'm not here to take anything from you. Happy birthday, by the way."

This seems to soften her a little bit. Mollified that Grass is safe, she takes Elyse and wanders away a few feet, leaving Eli and I alone.

With Aster not right underfoot, Eli works up the nerve to ask what he really wants to ask, "What happened to your face?"

"I can't tell you."

"Nellie, are you guys okay, I mean really okay?"

I have no idea how to answer that.

"We're not supposed to be talking to you."

"Who did this to you?"

I step backwards away from him, away from the draw he has on me. "We're not supposed to talk to you" I repeat. Like a fool I feel tears stinging my eyes. I want to go with him. I know instinctively he would never beat me and lock me in the woodshed. Jack and the cabin is the only life I know.

Afraid of my feelings, afraid of my reaction to Eli, I take Aster and Grass and we run into the woods.

Eli calls after us.

"Do not follow me. And do not come back." I yell.

I run away from Eli, run to the cabin and the strangers that will soon be there.

Run to future that I no longer understand.

Chapter 19

NELLIE

I'm relieved to see Jack isn't back yet when we return to the cabin. We never did get any berries and I set the empty berry basket back in the storage area. Aster seems like she's in a foul mood.

"What's wrong, baby?"

"I don't like new people."

"Do you mean Eli?" She nods and sticks her finger in her mouth. "How about we pretend we never saw him. Let's just make believe we went for a walk with Grass and the doll and nothing happened."

"Okay." Aster tucks the doll and Hoppy into her bed, then asks, "Why do these people want to come see me?"

"Just like Da-Da said, because you're the best girl in the world." Aster doesn't seem to believe my reasoning. Or maybe she's just reading the tension that radiates from me. I don't want these people to come see my daughter. There's no reason for it at least no good reason.

Aster and I finish off the last of the cake for lunch. We still have hours to wait before Jack returns with his friends and the tension and worry grows in my belly. The sky seems to share my apprehension as dark clouds gather beyond the trees. Soon large raindrops splatter the metal roof of the cabin making a lovely musical sound. We watch out the window as the approaching storm dumps buckets of water onto the front yard. As puddles form I think of an idea to distract us from the looming visitors.

"Want to swim in the rain?" Aster eagerly agrees, pulling her dress over her head and running out the cabin door into the downpour. Grass seems to love the idea as well and plods through the growing puddles splashing us both as she bounces around.

Rain baths are cleaner than creek ones and I have a suspicion that cleanliness will really matter to Jack tonight. I do wonder how he'll hide the injuries on my face from his friends. Probably tell them I fell down or ran into a tree.

I push the thought away and enjoy the time with Aster in the rain.

The sky rumbles and the rain pelts the grass, but over that sound I hear an approaching engine.

Aster is squealing and dancing with the dog and I tell her to be quiet. We both stand and listen. A sound from my past echoes through the trees.

The slamming of a car door.

Thoughts of the Maddison Militia flood my brain with panic. I grab Aster's hand and we run into the woods along the creek. I can only think of one place to hide, my hole in the dirt.

The flooding rain is already causing the creek level to rise. The entrance to my hole is only a few inches above the water level. I've never brought Aster here, have only come alone and only at night. The hole looks different in daylight. Aster climbs in with Grass, leaving little room for me. It's more important that she is hidden, so I sit on the edge.

Thoughts race through my head. "Did Eli tell on us? Has Jack and his friends already come and did they drive here?" I huddle in the entrance to the hole, hiding as much of my body as possible. Rain drips on half of my head, the droplets seeping through my hair causing me to shiver. We left our clothes at the cabin and the dirt scrapes my bare bottom as I try to wriggle closer into the hole. In the distance I hear someone calling my name.

It is not Jack. It is a voice I don't recognize.

The urge to sneak back towards the cabin and see who looks for me is strong. I hear my name again "Nellie, I won't hurt you. Nellie, are you here?"

I have no idea who the man is, why he is come here or how he has found us. I only know I must protect Aster. My curiosity gets the better of me. After instructing Aster to stay in the hole until I get back, no matter what, I make my way through the brush. As quietly as possible, crouching low to keep from being seen, I return towards the cabin. Standing in the grass between the cabin and the path I see a man in uniform. He turns and I duck to hide, laying flat on the ground. Sticks and leaves prick my bare skin as I peak around a bush. I can see his concerned face as he searches into the trees. He rubs his thick mustache, looks around the cabin yard then enters the cabin. He's inside for only a short time. Anxiety pounds at my heart the entire time I wait for him to return. I want to call to him to ask for help, but I stay silent.

Jack has trained me well.

The man may be in uniform, he may look like police, but the police are no more. The man must be an imposter. With one last search of the area the man goes back down the path towards his waiting vehicle. I breathe a sigh of relief knowing we are once again safe. The vehicle engine starts and soon the sound of it fades away.

I return to Aster.

She waits in the hole where I left her. Grass is digging at the soft dirt, her paws frantically tearing into the soil.

"Look, Mama," Aster says "Grass found bones."

Too much had happened in too short a time. My mind struggles to accept it all. Years of the quiet of the woods, of long empty days of nothing, of no other humans than Jack and Aster. Now two surprise visitors and more to come.

And Grass digging up bones.

Aster is so excited, thinking they must be animal bones or something similar. A toy of some kind for her to play with.

As Grass paws at the dirt, the unmistakable round shape of a skull begins to be unearthed. "Grass, stop that!" Thunder crashes around us and the rain falls harder. Naked and shivering I pull the dog away from the bones, pull Aster out of the hole.

"Get back to the cabin and dry off," I shout above the rumble and rain. Aster looks confused, but decides not to argue. She and

Grass take off into the trees.

My hole will never be a safe place again. I look at the two long bones and part of a skull uncovered in the hole. Part of one eye socket stares at me, accusing. This must be Anna.

I suddenly vomit into the creek. He killed her and buried her in the bank of the creek. The work of the water must have removed the loosened dirt, creating my safe haven hole. I want to vomit again. I'd been lying in that hole, inches from her.

Lying in a grave.

And taking solace in it.

With shaking hands, I cover the bones back up. I don't know what else to do. There's no one to tell about what we've found. If Jack finds out we know, he'll kill me too, possibly kill Aster. My world spins and dips, the very core of me shaken by all that has happened in the last few days.

A missing woman.

Scratches on Jack and then the dirt under his nails.

Robbed and then disappeared. The same

night he brought home the older lady clothes.

And the bag of stuff he wouldn't let me see.

I wish I could climb into the hole and let the earth drown all my fears and confusion. I can never go in my hole again.

It is a grave.

Chapter 20

SHERIFF KINGSLEY

Nellie shivers as she tells me this last part. I feel a twinge of surprise myself, even though I already knew what she'd find in that hole. I want to ask her more about the bones, but I'm letting her tell the story in her own way. We'll get to that part when the time is right.

"Why did you hide from me? I was only trying to make sure you were alright."

"I had no way of knowing that. I still don't know what you're intentions are with me right now. Jack always said not to trust others, especially those in uniform." She motions to my badge.

"Most of what Jack told you wasn't true."

"I only know that now. I didn't know for sure at the time."

We sit in silence for a few moment while she gets her thoughts in order. "What you need to understand is all of this happened very quickly. I spent years in that cabin. The first years with just Jack and his tales of the world. There was no more electricity, so we had no electricity. There were no more stores, so he scavenged for what he could find too feed us. He told me what he needed me to believe. I was just a girl, he was an adult. I trusted him. His reality became my reality."

"Meeting Eli changed that?"

Her cheeks turn pink under the dirt and the bruises. "Meeting Eli changed everything. I thought I could trust him, but once you showed up at the cabin, I knew he had told on us."

"He was concerned, that's why he came to me."

"Why was he so worried? Sure, I have a black eye, but that's none of his business. I begged him to leave us alone."

"When his friends told him about how Jolene Sparkman disappeared years ago, he grew curios and afraid she might be you. With Tonya Fredricks missing now the coincidence was too much. You should be thanking that young man."

She pulls her bare feet up onto her chair and wraps her arms around them. The scrapes on her knees are red and raw. She settles the doll between her legs and her chest. She looks like a frail child.

"Is he here?" she finally asks.

"He was. He went with the other kids to get sandwiches for everyone. Do you want to see him?"

She looks away, uncertain.

I leave the subject of Eli and try a different tactic.

"What did you think would happen when Jack brought his friends? You had to have some idea."

She swivels her head back in my direction, daring me with her eyes. Slowly, she puts first one foot back on the floor, then the other. In measured words she says, "If I knew what he planned, I would have taken Aster out of there right then."

"You really had no idea?"

"All I knew was what I had always known.

Do whatever it takes to keep Jack happy. He wanted to bring some friends to meet Aster. She's a lovely girl, why wouldn't they want to meet her? Besides after Grass found the bones, I was spooked hard. There was no way I was going against Jack's wishes after that. Not if I wanted a different fate than Anna's.

"How did you know the bones were Anna's?"

"I didn't really. But I assumed. He locked someone named Anna up in the woodshed. She wasn't there when I came to the cabin. The bones were buried along the creek near the cabin. You're a sheriff, you do the math."

"What did you do with the bones?"

"I covered them and tried to forget I ever saw them."

"How can you forget bones?"

"I had bigger things on my mind. Like keeping my daughter safe."

Chapter 21

NELLIE

Lightening crashes so close by, I feel a tingle on my bare skin. I need to get out of the storm. As I plod back to the cabin, I purposely shut the doors of my mind against all I have seen today. Against Eli coming. Against the police officer's arrival. Against the bones. None of that happened. None of that is real.

The only thing real is Jack will be back soon and he will want the cabin and Aster and I to be clean and presentable. Mud has splattered up my legs and I feel pieces of leaves in my hair. When I reach the part of the creek closest to the cabin, I call for Aster.

She runs out of the cabin, jumping as lightening cracks across the sky. "Come here and wash," I tell her.

"Rain bath."

"No, dunk under here and wash away the

dirt from the hole."

The rising water of the creek intimidates her and she hesitates. "Don't want to."

I lose my patience and snap, "Get in this water now and rinse the mud off."

Aster's lips quiver, not used to me being harsh. I'm not used to it either. My frayed nerves nearly snap as she bravely takes a step into the rushing creek.

Guilt swamps me as the water reaches her belly. Tears of shame course down my cheeks as I take her tiny body into my arms. She shivers there, stiff and scared.

"I'm so sorry I snapped, baby. I know you are frightened." Her hot face warms my bare shoulder. "Let's wash this mud off and then we'll go inside and get warmed up, okay."

She nods against me. We wash as quickly as possible then carefully make our way indoors. I continue my soft, reassuring voice as I dry her off and dress her in one of her cutest outfits. "There you go, the best little girl in the world."

I dry and dress myself in preparation for

Jack's return. In a sudden burst of rebellion, or as a test, I put on one of the bright floral shirts he brought home the night he was scratched. The night that woman was robbed and disappeared. Does this shirt belong to her?

The thought makes me shudder.

The doors to the cabin are shut tight against the storm. For once, the heat in the cabin is not insufferable. The afternoon draws into evening and I make Aster and I some dinner. As we eat, I tell her seriously how important it is to not mention seeing Eli or hiding in the hole or Grass finding the bones. "Just a game today. All of it was make believe. You will remember not to talk about it right?"

"I'll remember," she says solemnly. I hate that I'm begging her to lie, but fool myself that not mentioning something isn't the same as a lie. Keeping quiet to keep safe is not a lie.

"All of it is just make believe," I repeat, as much to convince myself as to convince her.

The rain has stopped and the sun is low in the sky by the time Jack returns. Aster, Grass,

Hoppy and Elyse and I are all piled into my bed and I'm telling them a story. Aster put Elyse on my lap, saying she likes me best. I find the weight of the doll on my lap comforting, sure I had hallucinated the dolls movements yesterday and forcing myself to believe the story of me putting her on the box accidentally. I was tired, I am tired. It could be true.

I hear Jack open the cabin door and I call out, "In here." His bulk soon fills the doorway of our bedroom.

"Hi, Da-Da, it's story time."

While Jack looks at Aster, I remove Elyse from my lap.

"This is a lovely scene." He looks at me, a flicker of surprise crosses his face. Was it from the shirt I'm wearing or from my bruises? When I'd checked the small mirror in the kitchen, my cheek was a dark purple and my eye was puffy and grey.

"Your face," he says. "It looks horrible."

Did he forget how I got the bruises?

"I know. I'm sorry." My blood sings with

anxiety, hoping Aster will remember to not mention the events of the day, hoping Jack won't fly into another rage because I am less than perfectly done up.

"My friends will be here soon." The words hang like a threat.

"What would you like us to do? I think I have some tea that I could make."

He flicks his eyes over my bruises again then tells Aster, "I need to talk to Mama outside for a moment. Why don't you put your toys away for me."

Aster immediately jumps off the bed to obey.

"I need Grass, too."

Jack wraps his hand around my wrist and pulls me off the bed. I can only follow. Aster watches warily from her cot as Jack takes me outside. He calls for Grass to follow. Grass growls low in her throat, her black hair raising on her neck. "Its okay, Grass. Come on girl." Warily, the dog follows.

Outside, Jack drops the pretense of nice and hisses in my ear. "You look like trash. Wearing an old lady's shirt and your face all messed up like that."

I want to point out that both the shirt and the bruises are from him. "I did the best I could."

"I did the best I could," he mocks in a sing song. Dragging me by my upper arm, he heads in a familiar direction. Towards the wood shed.

"I don't want my friends to see you like this."

"Why are they coming? What do they want with Aster?" I stammer as I struggle through the near dark, trying to keep up with Jack's quick pace.

"Better you don't know." He pauses outside the wood shed and turns the dial on the lock, squinting in the dark to see the white numbers. "You just stay in here and don't cause me any trouble and it will all be okay."

"They won't hurt her, will they? You'll keep her safe?" I let him put me in the shed. He laughs and shoves Grass in after me.

"She's my daughter. I'll do what I want with her." He shuts the door in my face and latches it closed.

"She's my daughter and I demand to know what you are doing with her!" My shouts don't faze him or slow him down. Agitated, Grass barks and growls at the door, not liking being locked in anymore than I do.

I press my eye to the gap, in the moonlight, I catch a glimpse of his back as he disappears into the trees.

Last time I was locked in here I was desperate to save myself, this time I'm desperate to save Aster. I fall to my knees and pray like I've never prayed before. Over and over, I pray to keep her safe, pray for a hedge of protection around her.

As time passes, I imagine all sorts of horrible things he might have planned for her. She is so young, so fragile. Too young for what he did to me when I first came to the cabin.

It suddenly dawns on me what a couple would want with a child. The best little girl in the world.

A sales pitch.

As realization dawns, I begin to scream her name. I scream over and over, hoping the couple can hear me, hoping I'll scare them away. She is my daughter, they cannot have her.

I scream and Grass barks.

Stopping to catch my breath and begin screaming for her again, I hear a small voice say, "I'm right here, Mama. Stop screaming. I came as fast as I could."

I collapse on the floor in relief. She's here. She's safe. At least safe for the moment.

"The lock is hanging loose, do you want me to open the door?"

"Yes, baby. Let us out."

As soon as the door swings wide, I pull my daughter into my arms. I mold her to me, pressing her so tight against me she begins to wiggle to be let down.

"You're hurting." I let her go and stand her up on the ground.

"Did they hurt you? Did they touch you? Are you okay? Where's Jack?" I fire questions at her.

"They were nice. The lady held me on her lap and let me tell her all about Hoppy and

Elyse and Grass. Da-Da said not to talk about you, so I didn't."

"You're a very good girl. What else did Da-Da say?"

"He and the man said a lot of numbers. The lady was nice. She smelled good."

"Are they all gone now? Jack and the couple."

"They left and I came to find you."

I tousle her lovely curls, so glad to have her next to me as we walk back to the cabin.

It is way past her bedtime when we return to the cabin. "Want to sleep in my bed tonight?" I ask. "You can bring all your toys and the dog."

She nods sleepily. I change her out of her fancy dress and into a nightgown. I toss the dress on the floor and stomp on it while she isn't looking. I can't believe I dressed her up like a prize. If I had been thinking clearly, I would have made her look as bad as possible.

All snuggled into my bed, I blow out the candle. I pull her close against my chest and wrap my body around her. She wriggles against the restraint. "Just for a few minutes.

Mama missed you."

Aster gives into the overbearing affection.

Her body twitches as she drifts towards sleep. I finally ask the question I've been dreading. "Did the couple or Jack say when they'd be back?"

"In a few days," Aster mumbles. "The woman said she'll bring me candy."

I bury my face into her hair and breathe deeply, drinking in the scent of her.

A few days.

As exhausted as I am, I lie awake with my daughter in my arms. I think of the bones in the hole and the name scratched in the wall. Did Jack do this to Anna? Did he steal her child then kill her? Will he sell Aster then bury me by the creek too?

Chapter 22

ELI

After seeing Nellie beat up, I couldn't keep my promise to not tell about her. I left the woods and went straight to the Sheriff. I'd seen him around Ella's mom's sandwich shop quite a few times. He was friendly for a sheriff, I thought I could trust him.

He didn't disappoint, but his finding did.

"I found a cabin," he says on the phone later that day, "I didn't find the girl or her child or a dog. Either that wasn't the right cabin or they weren't there."

"Do you think something happened to her? She was beat up and spooked."

The Sheriff Kingsley sighs heavily. "I'm not sure what else you want me to do here, Eli. It's not a crime to live in the woods. Unfortunately, unless she reports the injuries, there's nothing I can do about that either. For all I know, she's fine, or at least as fine as possible. If you have anything else to go on, I'll gladly follow up, but my hands are tied at the moment."

I hang up the phone dejected, my concern for Nellie not dissipated in the least. If the police won't help her, maybe my friends and I can do something.

After a round of texts, Noah, Ella and Faye all arrive at my house and are seated on my back patio where we have a good view of the woods in the distance.

I tell them every detail about Nellie and Aster and how they took Grass. I leave out the part about the doll named Elyse. I get the feeling it's a sore subject and not really the point of my meeting.

"What do you want us to do about it?" Faye asks, always the logical one. "If the sheriff hasn't found anything what can we do?"

"We could go to the cabin ourselves, poke around a bit," Noah offers, ready for an adventure.

Ella is quite in thought. "What do you think?" I ask her. She runs her hand through her dark hair slowly, thoughtfully.

"On the one hand, there's nothing to it. So a girl lives in the woods with her daughter. She could be prepper or and hippie type or who knows what." Ella looks at Noah with a pointed look. "On the other hand, there's Jolene Starkman."

Noah takes a sharp breath. "I hadn't thought of that," he says. "The age fits."

"Who's Jolene Starkman?" Faye and I say at the same time.

Noah takes over the story. "She was a girl that went to school with us. I didn't know her well, but in a school as small as ours, you kind of know everyone."

"I knew her a little. We had a few classes together in seventh grade."

"What does this Jolene have to do with Nellie?"

Noah gets to the point. "Jolene disappeared 5 years ago. She was twelve at the time. Her house burned down, killing her parents. She was never seen again."

Silence fills the patio and my eyes are drawn

to the woods. "What did Jolene look like?"

"Blonde curly hair. I think blue eyes or light brown," Ella supplies.

My mouth goes dry. "Nellie has blonde curls and blue eyes."

The four of us lose ourselves in the story, each afraid it could be true.

"What do we do?" I ask miserably. "I've already been to the sheriff. He's already found a cabin that might be where she lives. He says there's nothing else to be done right now."

"He hasn't put together that she could be Jolene." Noah says.

Faye has been quite, thinking, planning. "Ella, could your aunt help? She was a detective once."

Ella seems startled at the suggestion. "Maribeth? I mean, maybe," she hedges.

"We could at least ask her for advice. This Nellie could just be some innocent earth child or something, Maribeth would know what to do."

"She had a black eye and talked about a militia. There's something not right there," I say. "If your aunt can help, let's go." I stand, ready to save Nellie from whatever has her.

"Slow down," Faye says. "We'll go, but think about this. If this girl is Jolene and has been kidnapped for years, why didn't she run away to safety with you? She's obviously not being held captive if she's out looking for berries."

That sobers us all.

Ella get's to her feet. "Let's go talk to Maribeth. She'll know what to do."

Chapter 23

NELLIE

Even with Aster next to me, I have trouble sleeping. I feel worn and worried. If Jack has done what I think he's done, I only have a few days until the couple will come back for Aster.

What will happen to me then?

I think of Eli and how he made it sound that the world was not the torn military state that Jack made it out to be. Eli seemed nice, maybe we can leave here and go to him.

Do I have the bravery to leave? Maybe I'm reading the entire situation wrong.

I don't see any other way to read the situation. But I need more information.

Leaving Aster with Grass, I slip in the night. I wish I could go to my hole, to hide from all of this. Hiding won't save Aster or me. I walk towards the hole and past it. I search the trees for the red light on the grain mill. The only definite sign of civilization I remember from before my life in the cabin.

I lose sight of the light a few time, but keep in the direction and pick the trail up again. I march through the night, listening to the coyotes baying in the distance. The predators don't scare me. The truth is more terrifying.

After a while, the light grows larger, closer. It's late and the night is quiet, but I can hear vehicles. The trees suddenly open up to a dirt lane. The lane heads through the woods towards the light, so I follow it. Soon I reach the edge of the woods.

The lack of trees overhead startles me. For years, the trees have surrounded me, insulated me from the world. Beyond the trees, a field stretches to meet the back yards of several houses. Many of them have lights on. Flickering light pours out of one window. The recess of my brain remember the light as from a TV screen. The memory startles me. I'd forgotten TV existed. A woman crosses a window to what must be a kitchen sink. She seems to fill a glass with water and drink it.

TV, electricity, running water? Where is the desolation, the chaos the horrors that Jack has described for years?

Scared and more than a little freaked, I turn and run down the dirt lane, back to the trees, back past my hole by the creek. I run the entire way to the cabin and arrive with a huge stitch in my side and a hole in my heart. The sun is beginning to rise as I collapse on the back steps, desperate to catch my breath, desperate for my world to make sense again.

Jack has lied about everything.

Once I can breathe normally again, I look around the cabin and plan our escape. I have no idea if Eli will take us in or if we even can find him. I know the general direction he came to us from, east of the cabin. Beyond that, it's a mystery. I don't want to let Aster know what I'm planning, don't want to scare her until I have to. This cabin is the only life she knows. Plus she isn't too fond of Eli. I only hope after I get everything packed, she'll be willing to come with me. If not, I'll carry her kicking and screaming before I let Jack sell her.

Checking the food stores, I make a mental list of what to take with us. On the slight chance that the houses I saw were a fluke and the world is in some sort of mess, I want to be prepared. In case we need to fend for ourselves, I don't want to starve to death. I'm willing to steal and scavenge the way Jack does, but having some stock on hand would be beneficial.

I then make mental plans of what clothes and items of ours to take. We don't have much. I wish we had some valuables to trade if we need to. Aster is the only valuable thing in the cabin.

My mental lists made, I search for something to carry our small store of items in. Jack has the bags he takes on his trips. They would be perfect, but they aren't here. I'm in the bedroom removing pillow cases to use as carrying bags when I hear Aster exclaim, "Hi, Da-Da."

I quickly return the pillow to the pillow case, swearing under my breath. My plan to escape will have to wait.

I walk around the door jamb and face Jack. He picks Aster up and gives her some uncustomary attention. I half expect him to take her now, to carry her away from me and sell her to his friends. My eyes dart behind him, through the open door into the grass area between the cabin and the path to the world. Jack is alone. I breathe a sigh of relief. We can still escape, I just have to wait until he leaves again.

"Did you have a good night?" I ask in as normal a voice as I can. Normally when he is out all night, he comes home tired and worn, bags full. He's set the empty bags by the door and looks fresh and well rested.

"I did." He says simply. "I see Aster let you out of the shed. I didn't lock it on purpose. You know I could have." The warning is clear.

"But you love me and love her. You don't want to hurt us." The accusation is clear.

"There are things you don't understand about life beyond these walls, Nellie. It's best if you let me deal with it."

I now have some idea about that world, but I keep that tidbit of info to myself.

No matter what is beyond these walls, there's never a world where selling Aster is an option. Sensing the tension in the room, Aster wriggles to be let down. Jack sets her on her feet, but puts his hand on top of her head. A subtle threat. "Things could be worse," he says, closing his hand on her curls.

"Da-Da, you're hurting me," Aster pulls her head away from his grip. He releases her and she goes outside with Hoppy and Grass.

Tears sting my eyes at the implication that he would hurt her rather than sell her.

"I don't understand," I whisper. "I thought we were happy. What changed?" I hate myself for asking, for pleading for an answer.

"You changed."

I shake my head fervently. "I'm the same woman I was before. I'm yours always and forever. Why are you torturing me?"

He grins menacingly, "This isn't about you. You have no idea what life is like out there, I keep telling you that. It takes a lot of extra work to keep her fed and clothed. I can trade that hassle for something better."

"There is nothing better than her," I say miserably.

Jack shrugs. "That's what they think, too. That's what makes the deal so sweet."

"My daughter is not a deal, not something to be haggled over."

"My daughter is." He steps towards me and it takes all of my will power not to cower away from him. My stance surprises him. "See you changed."

Maybe he's right, just a few short days ago, I would never have stood up to him in any way. Is it my fault he's doing this?

"Do you want me to beg? I will, gladly. I'll do anything you want if you just call the deal off." I drop to my knees ready to plead my heart out until he relents.

"You can beg all you want, but the deal has already been made."

"Please, Jack, don't do this. She's all I have."

He looms over me, "I am all you need. I

should have eliminated the distraction years ago. See what you do to me, Nellie? You twist me up and get me to do your bidding."

"Because I love you and you love me." I'll say anything to make this stop.

"You love her more. You dote on her and she takes all your attention."

"I can change. I'll pay you more attention. I'll do anything you want, everything you need. Please just leave her be. She needs her mother."

"She'll have a new mother. Now get off the floor and stop groveling. Have some self-respect."

He might as well have slapped me, his words sting so badly.

That entire day and the next, Jack stayed home. The entire time, I can feel his eyes on me, watching for any sign of disloyalty, of deception. I'm good at playing the "keep Jack happy" game. I would win a blue ribbon for the way I played it those two days. He didn't have to ask for a thing. If he was hungry, I already had the food ready. If he was thirsty, I was offering him a drink before he could ask.

Things seemed almost like old times. Jack was happy. Aster was oblivious to the deadline hanging over her. I pretended to be happy, too.

Inside I was seething. And planning.

On the second afternoon, Jack takes Aster out to the front yard. I'm making Jack's favorite dinner and I watching from the window of the kitchen. I don't want to take my eyes off of my daughter, afraid he'll swoop her up and run down the path with her. There had been no mention of the upcoming deal. I want to fool myself that it was just a bad dream.

My heart won' let me fool myself about another thing.

"You could run out the back door towards Eli. You could be far away before he realizes you have gone."

The words are in my mind, but I turn my head as if someone has spoken them out loud. Elyse is on Aster's cot, her peeling, melted eye watching me.

"I can't leave without her." I say to the doll.

"You know there's only one way out of this."

"I've already thought of that. I'm not sure I can do it."

"After what he did to your family and to you? You can't do it for Aster?"

"I don't remember all that." It's only half-true. Pieces of my previous life have been slipping into my mind over the last days. Memories of my first weeks here, of the beatings and the unspeakable things he did to me.

"You do remember and he deserves to pay before it's too late."

I stare at Elyse across the room. Not sure if the words are coming from her or from somewhere deep inside me. Aster bounds in the front door right then, breaking the weird connection I have with the doll.

"Mama, Da-Da says the lady with the candy is coming tomorrow. I haven't had candy since Christmas."

Jack enters behind her, watching my face for a reaction. I don't give him the satisfaction of seeing me flinch. I smile blandly and say, "How lovely." To Jack, I say, "It might be nice to have some privacy here, after all."

The hardest lie I've said in the game so far.

Chapter 24

NELLIE

Aster has no idea what's coming, so she's happy and talkative at dinner. Jack keeps catching my eye as if to say, "See, she's a distraction."

I don't know how he can be so blasé about the situation. It's the last night our daughter will be with us, and he's acting as if it's just a normal night.

I am too, but I'm definitely acting. I'm focusing all my attention on him, pretending I've come around to his way of thinking. Pretending I'm okay with selling my child.

"Is there anything special you want in exchange for," I nod to Aster. "Something you've been wanting." The words burn my tongue, but I force myself to sound pleasant as if the deal is done.

"I've had my eye on a few things. I was

thinking maybe get a generator for here. We could have lights instead of candles. Even a small stove instead of a wood burner."

"Ooh, I'd like that. You are so thoughtful."

Stupid Jack falls for my act.

"What are lights?" Aster asks.

Jack meets my eye as if saying again, "Told you so."

"Nothing you need to worry about, baby. If you're done eating, why don't you go out and play until bed time."

Aster bounces out of her chair and goes outside.

"I was thinking maybe we could play tonight at bedtime, too." I say in my most seductive voice. Bile rises at the back of my throat as I say the words.

Jack looks surprised, but excited at the prospect. "Is it dark yet?" he jokes.

"It will be soon." I stand and start clearing the table. "Maybe I'll wear that nightgown and the shoes you brought home last time." I have to turn away from his look of interest before I lose my dinner all over the table.

"Stick with the plan. You're doing fine."

Elyse's words or mine, I keep going. "I enjoyed that."

He's suddenly behind me, his hands gripping my shoulders. "This better not be a trick," he hisses in my ear. "No matter what you do, I will not change my mind about tomorrow."

I turn to face him and wrap my arms around his waist. "No trick. I'm just grateful that you want to get lights and a stove for the cabin, and I want to show you. I keep telling you I love you more than anything."

"More than Aster?"

I can't force my mouth to say the words, so I nod against his chest.

"Put her to bed early and you can show me how much."

I swallow hard at the sick taste in my mouth. "Just let me finish cleaning up the kitchen."

Jack smacks me on the rear playfully and goes outside. As I wipe the diner dishes clean, I watch him, judging his movements, looking to be sure he believes me.

"Well done."

I hum under my breath as I clean and plan. "The farmer takes a wife, the farmer takes a wife, hi-ho the dairy-o the farmer takes a wife."

I'm filled with exhilaration at what is to come. Not the interlude I promised Jack, that is just a necessary evil. What happens afterwards is all that matters.

I look out the window again to make sure he and Aster are still busy outside. They are throwing Grass a stick and letting her bring it back. Aster laughs like she doesn't have a care in the world. As far as she knows, she doesn't.

I check under her cot for the extra pillow case I stashed there earlier. Jack rarely ever goes into the storage area where her cot is, and he has no reason to look under her bed. The case holds what we'll need if my plan works. If it doesn't, we'll both be dead. I pull the twine I hid there out of the bag and sit it next to it for easy access.

"Lord, please forgive me for what I am about to do. Place a hedge of protection around us, at least around Aster. I may no longer deserve your protection."

Elyse is on the bed, eyelevel with me. I swear the doll nods at me, cheering me on.

I no longer care about my sanity.

I only care about making Jack pay.

It takes every ounce of will power I posses to participate enthusiastically in the ruse I set up. I dressed in the nightgown and heels, I played the part he desired of me. I did everything required of me with an uncharacteristic appearance of enjoyment.

Jack fell for it all.

When it was finally over and he rolled off of me, I mentally prepared for the next step. Believe it or not, getting him into bed was the easy part of my plan. I survived the degradation just as I have always survived. At least this time it served a purpose.

"Phew," Jack says breathlessly. "That was something else." He throws an arm over his head and pulls me against his bare chest. He is slick with sweat and it stings the nearly healed cut on my cheek. I wait until his breathing has slowed into a regular rhythm and he is asleep until I pull away from him.

"Where are you going?" he asks sleepily.

"Outhouse," I whisper, making the foul word sound as seductive as possible. "I'll be right back."

I wait until his breathing slows again and I'm fairly sure he's asleep before I scoot to the end of the bed. I grab the t-shirt and shorts I purposely left there and dress as quietly as possible. Thankful for the covering of clothes, I then sneak out of the room and shut the door.

There is only a sliver of moon tonight and the cabin is unusually dark, feeling my way, I light a small candle. The light illuminates Aster's open eyes.

I hold a finger to my lips to tell her to be quiet as I walk to her.

"Did Da-Da hurt you again?" she asks. With a start I realize that she heard everything we did through the thin wall between our beds. Right now I can hear Jack snoring on the other side. I never realized how much Aster could hear. The though makes me cringe.

"Shh, we are going for a trip. Isn't that exciting?"

"Elyse says we can't go yet. She says Da-Da must pay."

I stare at my daughter in shock. I'm sure Elyse didn't tell her anything, the thought came from Aster's own mind.

The question slips from my lips, "Pay how?"

Slowly, Aster turns her head to stare at the box high on the shelf.

I don't know exactly what Aster has in mind, but I like the idea of making Jack suffer by destroying his disgusting box of animal bones.

I slide the pillow case out from under her bed, then change her from her nightgown to a pair of shorts and t-shirt. Her eyes follow every movement I make, anxious and excited and just a bit drowsy.

I check to make sure Jack is still snoring then tell Aster, "Wait right here with Grass until I come to get you."

Her brown eyes are huge in the candlelight,

but she agrees to wait.

Jack's snoring loses its rhythm and I freeze afraid he woke up. A moment later, he snores again, sound asleep.

"If you hear mama yell, I want you to run. Run towards where we met Eli. Take this bag with you."

"I'm scared," she whispers to Elyse. A dreamy look comes over her eyes. "You're going to hurt him, right?"

"Only if I have to."

I kiss the top of her head then take the twine, grab a knife from the kitchen and re-enter the bedroom.

Thankfully, Jack is on his back, his arms and legs spread across the bed. I say a quick prayer to God that he won't wake up. I'm not sure that God will approve of the prayer, but I say it anyway. Jack has always been a deep sleeper, and I hope he sleeps well after all I just did to him.

Inch by inch, I slide the twine under his wrist, then wrap the end of it around the bed post. I tie the knot tight and cut the twine with the small kitchen knife.

He snores on.

The other wrist will be trickier as I have to lean over him to get to it.

Holding my breath, I slip the twin under his arm, then reach for the bedpost. My breasts accidentally brush against his face as I maneuver the length of twine around the far bedpost.

"Mmm," he moans against my skin.

I freeze and fight the urge to scream in disgust. I hang there over him waiting for his snoring to start again. He mumbles my name, then snores on.

With both of his hands tied out of the way, I feel a little more bold, a little safer.

The plan will work. We can escape without him following.

I slowly move myself off of him, preparing to tie his legs in the same way.

His snoring suddenly stops.

"What the hell?" He suddenly shouts. He pulls on his hands and for a moment I worry the ties won't hold. He pulls and twists, but he can't escape the bed.

The room suddenly lights up as Aster enters the room with the candle. Jack pulls at the bindings, kicks at me with his free legs.

The twine holds.

"You will not get my daughter, you bastard," I hiss. I lay across his legs as he kicks and fights back. I manage to wrap the twine around both ankles and make some semblance of a knot. His feet are tied together.

Aster hasn't said a word, just watches with Elyse in one arm and the candle in the other hand. Grass stands next to her, hair hackles raised and prepared for battle if needed.

"Let's go," I tell her.

As if in a trance, Aster approaches the bed where Jack is writhing and fighting to get loose. Aster holds the candle close to his face. He stops yelling and tries to move way. The flame catches his sparse hair and the smell of it singing fills the room.

I make a move to stop her.

"Let her do it. You know you want her to."

I do want her to. I want her to hurt him as

much as he's hurt us. Aster pulls the candle away from his hair, looks down at Elyse then looks over her shoulder at me. I barely recognize my daughter.

"The box, Mama." She sounds other-worldy, her eyes larger than I've ever seen them.

"Make him pay."

I hurry into the kitchen and grab the offensive box off the shelf. Aster is holding the candle close to Jack's face again when I return to the bedroom. She has sat Elyse on his tied legs. Jack stares at the doll in wonder. He doesn't try to kick her off, only stares as if he's entranced like Aster is.

"The farmer took a wife, and a child," Aster says. "He never sold that child. You planned to sell Aster."

"I would never," Jack scrambles to lie, to calm the demon that has overcome his daughter.

"Don't lie to me," Aster croaks in a voice not her own. "You were going to sell her and they were going to do unspeakable things to her."

I watch and listen in horror. "You said they wanted a daughter, you said she'd have a new mama." I accuse the tied up man, pitiful on the bed, half his hair burned off.

"It was all a joke. I just wanted to see what you'd do." He turns his burned face to me, pleading. Only then does he see I'm holding his precious box.

Break it, smash it, spread the bones.

"You leave my box alone!"

"You no longer get to tell me what to do." With all the strength I have I throw the box against the wall. The wood splinters and bone fragments scatter over Jack on the bed. He howls in anger. The bones flicker yellow in the candle light. Now that I can see them clearly, I realize they are not animal bones at all. I recognize fingers and part of a hip.

"Oh my God," I whisper. "Those are human."

"Those are mine. Just get out. Just leave and never come back," he pleads.

Aster looks at Elyse's perch on Jack's legs, the slowly looks at me. She seems to ask me a question that I don't understand.

As if against her will, she holds the candle to the bed sheet hanging down. It only takes a moment for the fabric to catch fire. Jack screams in pain and fear. "Nellie, don't let her do this," he pleads.

Over the past few days, the memories of how I came to live in the cabin have been flickering into my mind. Seeing the spreading orange flames, the last part of how I got here snaps into place.

I lean close so he can hear me. "You burned my parents in their bed, why would I save you now?"

His eyes grow wide and he opens his mouth to say something. I take one of the bones and shove it into his open mouth to shut him up. "You've told enough lies. I don't want to listen to more."

I say, "We have to go," as I turn to Aster Aster is no longer in the room.

Chapter 25

NELLIE

I search the cabin for Aster as the flames in the bedroom grow. The smoke is starting to fill the rooms and I choke against the horrid smell. The burning in my chest feels too familiar. Jack taking me out of the window as my house burns runs through my mind. I'd trusted him. I'd thought he saved me.

He killed my family to have me.

I don't have time to think of that now, I need to find Aster. She's not under the kitchen table and she's not in her bed. As I cough I see Grass sitting next to the cot. I hurry across the plank floor and drop to my knees. I toss up the blanket and peer under the cot.

Aster huddles in the corner with Elyse clutched tight in her arms.

I reach for my daughter, begging her to come out.

Her scared eyes meet mine from under the low bed. "I didn't mean to do it, Mama. She made me do it."

If Elyse is talking to Aster the way she's talking to me, I can imagine how terrified she must be. I'd be freaking out if I gave myself half a chance.

"I know, baby. We can't think of that right now, we have to get out of here."

I reach for her and grab Elyse's dress instead. That will have to do. I pull, and Aster slides out with the doll.

I pull them both close then run for the front door.

The small sliver of moon offers little light as we run into the dark. Behind us I hear Jack screaming in pain. I trip over a log, taking Aster down with me. As we scramble back to our feet, the sky suddenly brightens as the cabin burns bright.

Grass whines next to us, uncertain of the change in events.

The flames reach the windows and out the open door.

Flames. Fire. An open window.

The night Jack kidnapped me snaps back into my mind in one solid memory.

I turn towards the burning cabin and scream in fury. "You killed my family, you shit! You stole me from my life. You don't deserve to live." The words turn to sounds of deeply hidden pain.

Aster takes my hand and turns me from the sight of the burning cabin. "Let's go."

We walk into the woods, now illuminated by the fire. There's no reason to hurry, Jack has stopped screaming.

We trudge near the creek in the direction I think Eli may live, the only person I know to go to for help. We could have taken the path that Jack always takes out of the woods, but I don't trust it. I don't trust anything that man has touched.

Our shadows stretch before us, one for me, one for Grass and one for Aster. Suddenly a fourth shadow springs on us.

"Thought you could tie me up, light me on fire and run away?" Jack howls as he grabs my hair. Broken twine hangs from his wrists. In the light of the fire I see most of his hair is missing and half his face is burned.

He reminds me of Elyse.

I twist and turn to escape his grip, sliding into the muddy bank of the creek, but he pummels me in the face, then kicks me in the gut. I fall to the ground and he lands on top of me. His fingers search for my throat and find a hold. I flail wildly with my hands searching the ground for something to use as a weapon.

My hand closes on a rock.

With a wide swing, I hit him in the side of the head with the rock.

Jack falls sideways onto the ground and I push away from him.

Jack moans and makes to get up, but Grass pounces and locks her jaws on his leg.

His howl of pain fills the night, he scrambles to keep fighting and manages to hit my head with a good wallop to the temple with his fist.

Aster has been watching all this in the quiet, almost hypnotic way she had with the candle. With slow, deliberate movements, she holds

Elyse over his head.

"You hurt mama," she says, then slams her into his face.

She then pounces onto his chest, and holds the doll hard over his mouth.

I should make her stop.

"But you don't want to."

I don't want to. Instead, I kick him in the head. Aster holds the doll against him a moment longer.

Jack stops kicking.

Stops breathing.

Aster looks up at me, the flames reflecting in her huge eyes. I've never seen her so wild.

I reach my hand to her and help her up from her dead father's body. Grass senses there's no fight left in him and releases his leg.

Breathing hard, I look down at the man that held me captive for so many years. The man who destroyed all I loved. The man who took my innocence and replaced it with degredation.

"Smash him."

I don't even try to fight her suggestion. I grab the rock and start slamming it into his face. I wail and scream as I hit him, releasing the years of pent up frustration and fear. I smash again and again.

His hot blood spatters on my face, runs down my hands and covers my t-shirt.

I smash until he is no longer recognizable.

Falling onto the ground, I drop the rock. I then lay on my side on the ground and watch the fire burn the cabin, red-orange fingers raking the trees. I cry in relief and shame, unable to form a thought, unable to do anything other than feel.

Aster climbs over to me, "Mama?" she puts her hands on my shoulder and I turn my face to her. She recoils at the sight.

"Mama, bloody." My normally talkative child has been shocked into few words.

Something cracks near us and Grass growls. I sit up, ready to do battle if needed.

A coyote wanders into the light of the fire. It locks eyes with me, then raises its head and bays to the sliver of moon.

The forlorn sound breaks my heart.

In the distance another coyote howls in

response.

Grass howls too.

I tip my head back, close my eyes and howl along with the animals.

So does Aster.

We howl until my throat hurts. When I open my eyes again, the coyote is gone.

Amidst the orange glow of the cabin on fire, I see a ball of light hovering near us. My tired mind first thinks it's a firefly, but it's the wrong color and size.

Aster seems to listen to the light, then looks at me excitedly. "Benny says we need to go this way."

When I blink, the light is gone. "How does your bunny know the way?"

"Not my bunny. Benny."

I'm hurt and scared and confused. "Who is Benny?"

"The little boy that was just here. He says to follow him and he'll lead us to safety."

If Aster wants to imagine a little boy is leading us, then so be it. A moment ago we were howling with coyotes. With one hand pressed to my forehead and the other holding the pillowcase of everything we own in the world. I let my three year old daughter lead us into the night. Following the ghost of a young boy.

We walk for what seems like hours. Every so often, Aster pipes in with news from "Benny." Turn here, watch out for that hole, the pond is coming up on our right, that sort of thing. Freakishly, all of "Benny's" directions and warning turned out to be true.

"Just a little further and we'll be there," Aster says.

"Where are we going exactly? This isn't the way to where we met Eli, we left that direction long ago."

"Benny is taking us to his mom."

I stop walking. "Baby, who is Benny?"

"I told you. He's the little boy. He's right there."

While we have been walking the odd ball of light has appeared and disappeared. My tired mind said it was a fire fly. Now I see a ball of white light, not the yellow green of a bug. The ball turns into the shape of a little boy.

He beckons me to follow, then turns back into light.

My head aches and I sway unbalanced.

"See?" Aster says, then follows Benny into the dark.

I hurry to keep up.

Several minutes later a different kind of light shines through the trees. Electric light. On the breeze I hear a woman singing, "The wife takes a child, the wife takes a child."

Aster joins in the song.

We approach a cabin with a porch light on. A woman sits in a rocking chair, singing and rocking and seemingly waiting for us. A large gray husky sits on the porch next to her. She continues the song, not surprised at all to see us. Aster sings loudly. She turns and hands me the doll. "Elyse wants to be yours now," Then walks up to the woman on the porch as brave as can be. Grass goes with her and the two dogs sniff each other.

I hide in the shadows.

"It's okay," the woman says.

"Who are you?" I ask, holding the doll tight to my chest.

"My name is Maribeth Johansen. Benny was my son. He brought you to me."

Aster waits at the bottom of the porch steps, beckoning to me to join her. "Come, mama."

"It's over. You are safe now."

I look at the doll and back to Aster.

I step out of the shadows and into the bright light of Maribeth Johansen's porch.

"You're all bloody. Why don't you sit with me and tell me what happened."

I don't want to tell her. I don't even want to remember.

"My name is Jolene Starkman." The words sound both foreign and fitting on my tongue.

"Of course it is. I've already called Sheriff Kingsley once Benny told me you were coming. He's a brave boy. He hates the dark, but he went all the way to you to lead you here."

"I don't understand."

"Many things in Maddison, Indiana are hard to understand."

I walk up three steps to her porch and take the empty wooden rocking chair next to her. The wood creaks slightly under my weight. I sit the pillow case on the floor then pull Aster onto my lap and lean back in the chair. Tension leaves my body and I begin to weep quietly.

"Here, darling, let me take her." Maribeth allows Aster onto her own lap. Aster wraps her arms around her neck as if she will never let go. "I once had a little girl like you," Maribeth says. "Her name was Lilly."

"What happened to her?" Aster says.

"She died. Now she's like Benny. Although I haven't seen her in many months."

Maribeth reaches for my hand and gives it a squeeze. "I haven't seen Benny, either. You must be very important for him to come back for. Thank you for letting me see him for a moment."

Tears of relief and exhaustion roll down my cheeks and my mind is a muddle, but I wonder at the woman's sanity.

She laughs and the notes are sweet and lovely, not sharp and wild. "Don't worry, I haven't lost my mind. I'm a lot more sane now than I was, although sometimes my sister wonders."

A few notes of nervous laughter escape my lips. "You said you called the Sheriff? Does that mean there is no Militia?"

She looks at me quizzically. "What do you mean?"

"And these electric lights, do you have a generator somewhere?" I know the answers, know Jack lied about it all, but I need someone to tell me the truth.

"Oh dear, what did he do to you?"

I shudder at her concern. "He can't hurt us anymore. Is the world really in chaos, no money, no rules, nothing like before?"

"The chaos isn't any worse than it has always been. Is that what he told you?"

I can only nod, the enormity of Jack's deception overwhelming me.

We sit in companionable silence as we wait for the sheriff to arrive. Aster has curled into a ball on the woman's lap. She looks beautiful in the porch light. Nothing like the little girl smothering her father with a doll.

"How do you know who I am?" I finally ask.

"Everyone has been looking for you for a long time."

This breaks whatever dam I have inside and I cry wracking sobs. I haven't been alone. I just didn't know they were looking.

She hands me a tissue once I'm spent. "Clean yourself up a little. The calvary is here."

Swirling red and blue lights are making their way through the woods to the cabin. I go stiff with fear. "They are the good guys," she says.

I nod stiffly.

"I also called my sister, Nicole. I hope that's okay. I have trouble leaving my property, a severe form of social phobia, I guess. Anyway, I want to go to the station with you, but I don't think I can without Nicole."

"You don't seem like the kind of person that wouldn't be able to do anything," I say with surprise.

"We all have our limitations."

"Can we find my friend, Eli? He's been worried about me."

She blinks in surprise. "You don't know the half of it."

We don't have time to discuss it further. The police car has parked in front of the porch and the dark skinned man that I saw at the cabin a few days ago climbs the three steps to join us on the porch.

"Johansen," he says nodding to the odd woman. His eyes land on me. "Are you okay, miss?"

"I will be."

Chapter 26

KINGSLEY

As she finishes her story, I have to sit back in my chair. My throat is suddenly dry. I take the last water bottle on the table and drink half of it in one gulp. Several months ago, I wouldn't have believed some of the parts of her story, but I've seen a lot since then. Even looking past the fantastical parts, there's a lot to unpack.

Nellie stares at me, her chin high, defying me to not believe her. She holds the doll to her chest and it stares at me with its melted, peeling eye.

The murder weapon.

Well, not murder exactly. The self-defense weapon?

"You know this is a mess, right?" I finally say. "You could be in a lot of trouble here. Or Aster could be."

"Aster has nothing to do with it."

"She started the bed on fire with Jack tied to it. That's attempted murder."

Loaded silence fills the room. "She didn't know that. She didn't know what she was doing. She's only three."

"You knew."

"Then arrest me. Leave Aster alone."

"I don't think it's that easy."

"It can be as easy as you make it."

"I have a duty."

"I had a duty to keep my daughter safe. He was going to sell her. Like a piece of meat or a toy. *Sell* her."

"You make it sound so simple. You two killed him. There has to be justice."

"There is justice now. Justice for my family he murdered, for Anna he buried at the creek, for the missing woman he probably killed and buried somewhere. Who knows what other awful things he's done."

I slowly drink the rest of the water as I think about what she said and the implications.

"You already told me Aster lit the bed on

fire and then later smothered him with the doll."

She stares me down with her intense blue eyes. I fight the urge to flinch away.

"No I didn't. Don't put words into my mouth."

My own mouth falls open. So this is how she's going to play it.

"Next you'll say a ghost led us out of the woods to Maribeth's."

I'm conscious of the video camera in the corner, of the tape player on the desk. All of her statement has been recorded. It's all on record.

But her statement is crazy.

"If that isn't what happened, then tell me how it actually went down."

She sits back in her chair, holds the doll close under her chin. "I needed to escape with Aster so I tied him to the bed and we left. He must have gotten loose. A knocked over candle started a fire, because the cabin burned. Next thing I know, he attacked me. He pinned me to the ground and had his hands on my throat.

The dog tried to help and bit his leg. While he was distracted, I found a rock and hit him in the head with it. When he fell over, Aster and I ran into the woods to escape."

I look at her in amazement. This story matches the evidence. It makes more sense than a pre-schooler that was possessed by the spirit of a doll did the things Nellie said she did.

"Is that how it really happened?"

"I swear, every word is true."

Technically, every word was true. Was her first story just a figment of her overworked mind? After living through all she has been through, can I believe most of what she tells me?

"Are you willing to sign an affidavit to the validity of your statement?"

She blinks in confusion.

"Will you sign that all of this is true?"

She gives me a slow smile. "Of course it's all true. I'll sign whatever you need."

I take the affidavit off my clipboard and slide it across the table to her with a pen. She gives it a cursory look and picks up the pen. She signs "Nellie" and clicks the pen closed.

"If you don't have any more questions, I'd like to go see Aster. You said Eli and his friends were bringing food."

"They should be back by now. Are you hungry?"

"I'm starving."

She stands and walks to the door. "I'm free to leave, right?"

"I'm sure I will have lots more questions later, but you are free to go right now."

"Good, I've spent enough time in a cage."

After she leaves, I stare at the closed door a moment. Her story swirls through my mind, parts of it too fantastical to believe. The young woman that walked out of this room is so different than the scared girl I brought in here.

How much of it is true?

A knock on the door startles me from my contemplation of the girl. "Come."

It's Deputy Dallmeyer and Deputy Paxton. "I have the preliminary report of what we found at the scene of the fire for you," Paxton says.

"Hit me with it."

"The bones the girl mentioned were found buried next to the creek just as she said they were. Only a few inches below the floor of the hole or cave or whatever that was."

"A wash out," I provide the word to the flustered deputy.

"We'll need dental records to confirm, but the coroner said the bones are consistent with a female between the age of 15 and 25. Most likely she's Annabelle Hartman that went missing about twelve years ago from Draper Falls. Like I said we need dental records to confirm."

"Tell him about the jars," Dallmeyer interrupts.

Paxton gives him a withering look. "I'm getting to it." The deputy takes the seat Nellie had filled the last few hours. "First I want to tell him about what the dogs found. Cadaver dogs were brought out to search. At the entry to the path that led to the cabin, we found

Jack's truck. He must have kept it there and walked to the cabin so Nellie wouldn't know. The dogs did a search starting with the truck. They found a fresh shallow grave a few hundred yards into the woods. Decomp is minimal and the victim matches pictures of Tonya Fredrickson."

"So he did kill her."

"The jars," Dallmeyer interrupts Paxton.

Paxton does his best to control his reaction to Dallmeyer. "You can tell him," he finally says.

"The cabinet in the woodshed was full of jars."

I stare at him in confusion. "So?"

"Jars with things in them." Dallmeyer is enjoying this. I'm not.

"What kinds of things?"

"Jars of body parts. Fingers, toes, a tongue."

I look to Paxton for confirmation, my stomach roiling at the thought.

Dallmeyer is shifting his weight back and forth in excitement. "And get this. We found similar jars in Tonya's basement. Not with body parts, at least not human ones. One of them had the nose of a pig in it." He sounds way too interested.

"Specimen jars, the kind with formaldehyde in them," Paxton offers.

"Jars of things?"

The End

A note from Dawn Merriman:

Wow! This book was a whole different level of creepy for me. I loved writing Nellie and Aster's parts, but Jack – yuck! I knew he would get what was coming to him in the end, so I carried on.

This book was a bit different for me in another way as well. The first half I wrote my usual way. Then we had a small house fire and everything besides dealing with that and working on the house stopped. I had no energy left for creating, especially creating such a messed up world as the one Nellie lived in. I took about a month off from the book, with a day or two here and there that I tried to get some writing done.

Then life after the fire freed up a bit and I had the creative juices flowing again. I had a tremendous opportunity to do a "writer's retreat" come my way. My husband, kids and mother-in-law went out of town for a long weekend. I had four days all alone, and my mother-in-laws empty lake cottage to spend them in.

It was some of the best days of my life. Me, Nico my little dog, the lake and the book. Nothing else. For the first two days, all I did was write. It was amazing. I'd write a chapter or two, then nap, then write, then nap. I lived and breathed the book, something I'd dreamed of doing.

Before I knew it, the book was finished!

I still had a day and a half left of my retreat, but no book to write. I did a lot of planning for new books, (spoiler alert, there may be a new Gabby book in the making this year). I outlined a lot of murder plots. I "wrote" stories until my creative brain was drained.

Only then did I go home. With the rough draft of Cage on my hard drive and outlines note for future books.

So this book was a bit of slow and steady and then a full out sprint. However the words got on the page, I hope you enjoyed them.

I realize there are some loose ends not tied up with this book. That is by design. I tried to give you a satisfying story that stands alone, but also tie in the other books in the series as well as set you up with what you'll need to really sink your reader mind into the next book. "Jars of Things" should be released late 2021, or maybe early 2022. It will be the final book in the Maddison, Indiana Supernatural Thrillers series and should answer all of your hanging questions (if I do my job right). What's with the boxes of bones? Will Kingsley ever tell Nicole he loves her? Will Maribeth overcome her extreme social phobia? Will Elyse ever stop being such a creepy doll? Will the big bad thing in Maddison finally be beaten? WHAT's UP WITH THE JARS? So many things to put in one book.

Hope you are enjoying this series. Thank you for being such a loyal reader.

You can always join my newsletter at DawnMerriman.com. You can also join my Facebook Fan Club.

Until next time, happy reading.

God Bless,

Dawn Merriman

www.DawnMerriman.com

Printed in Great Britain
by Amazon

62688829R00151